THE MIDLIFE PRELUDE

PACKLESS IN SEATTLE, BOOK 1

LIA DAVIS

The Midlife Prelude

Published by Davis Raynes Publishing Group, LLC

PO Box 224

Middleburg, FL 32050

DavisRaynesPublishing.com

Cover by Glowing Moon Designs

Formatting by Glowing Moon Designs

DavisRaynesPublishing.com

ABOUT A MIDLIFE PRELUDE

Omega wolf shifter, Matilda Carol, is about to change her life forever. Starting over at forty-five isn't the scariest thing she'll have to face in her new life. But she'll pay any price to gain her independence. Even if it means she has to die in the process.

Faking her own death and moving away from the only home she's ever known is intimidating, to say the least. Especially when Mattie has been sheltered and controlled by her uncle all her life. It's a good thing that her BFF, Julie, is a powerful fae with connections to several paranormal factions that have all sworn to keep Mattie hidden from her uncle.

When Julie goes missing, Mattie will not rest until she's brought home. But she's never investigated a missing persons case before—or any other case.

When the police can't find any trace of Julie, Mattie does her own detective work with the help of a vampire king, a witch, and a mysterious hottie who stirs her inner wolf's mating urge. Wow. She didn't see that one coming.

Mattie may be packless in Seattle, but she's in control of her own destiny for the first time in her life. She's not about to waste this opportunity.

CHAPTER ONE

"I'm having doubts. What if something goes wrong?" I cringed at the sound of my own voice. It was whiney and even to me, I sounded like a pup doing something her mother told she had to do when I really didn't want to do it. I wasn't a pup—far from it—and it wasn't my mother telling me what to do. It was my best friend with the demands.

Actually, demands might be too strong of a description of our plan. Yes, *our* plan.

I was about to do something that went so far beyond my natural instincts that I wasn't sure I'd ever recover. But it was either me or my betrothed. One of us had to die. I didn't want to leave this earth just yet.

But my bestie said both of us had to go.

Of course, I'd be faking my death, or Julie would be while framing the mean SOB who my uncle insisted that I mated. Roger—my uncle—still thought of me as a pup and a piece of property that he could sell off to the highest bidder. I was forty-five years old, damn it! And more than capable in finding my own mate and living my own life. But no one in the Claws Creek Pack did anything without the Alpha's permission. Roger's word was law, no matter how cruel the command.

Faking my death was my only way out. At least I kept telling myself that. The reality of my situation wasn't so cut and dry. Roger wasn't only my uncle, he was my Alpha. The latter was something he reminded me of every day of my life since my mother died when I was fourteen.

It was hard to be the independent dominant female when he used his power to force me into submission. The fact that I was unable to shift into my wolf form made me the omega of the pack. The weakest link. The one that had to deal with all the mean girls, and guys, of the pack. Really, I was surprised I survived as long as I had.

Being sold off to another Alpha that was more of a sadist than Roger, put the fear of the Fates into me.

"You are better than that asshat of an uncle of yours. He is no Alpha. He's an insane, greedy rogue. The same goes for that bastard he sold you to." Julie's words were spoken through her teeth since she was trying to keep her anger and her voice on the down low so no one overheard our conversation. That was the reason we picked this diner, just outside of town—outside of Roger's territory. It was a human-owned place, meaning none of my packmates would be there. They were too good to hang out with humans. Especially eat with them. Besides not many of them left their own territory.

I shrugged and traced the rim of my glass. Julie and I had the day off. We worked at a bar and grill in town. Well, had worked. After tonight we wouldn't be back. "It's the fact that I'll be leaving Abbotsford. I've lived here all my life." And I'd never been outside of Canada. "Why are we going to Seattle?"

I knew why, but I wanted to hear Julie say it out loud. Felix, her ex-boyfriend-almost mate lived there. He was also the vampire who ruled the United States Pacific northwest.

"You know why," Julie said with a raised brow and smirk. "Felix can protect you there. No para-normal being enters his territory without him knowing. Not one. And believe me there have been idiots who tried. And died."

The thing Julie wouldn't admit to was that she was still in love with Felix. When I asked her why she hadn't moved with him when he was voted into as ruler of his region, Julie gave me the same excuse. "I don't fit in with royalty and politics."

That was a load of cat yak. She was born to be a queen and to rule. Literally, she was a fae princess and would have ruled her realm if war hadn't destroyed it a few years after she was born.

Julie looked at her phone, then slid it across the table to me. "It's time."

I handed her my cell and pocketed hers as I stood. Then we went into the restroom and switched clothes. It was important that she smelled like me as well as look like me. It wasn't unusual for her scent to be on me since we worked together.

After dressing, I pulled her hoodie over my head. "Be careful."

She winked at me. "Always. Call me when you get to the apartment and leave a message. I'll have the phone on silence with the vibrator turn off."

Precautions. I hated that we'd be out of touch for any period of time. It was for the better, or it would be if we pull this thing off.

Without another word, I tugged the front of my hoodie down to cover my face and stepped out of the diner. I made myself as small as I could as I moved through the crowded sidewalk. It was technique I had mastered at a young age, being the omega and all.

Right now, the less people saw of me the safer they all were. I was about to disappear and in a few hours I'd be dead. At least those who knew me would think I was dead.

The sound of metal crunching and glass breaking, startle me along with everyone on the sidewalk. Jerking my head up, I spotted a car that had smashed into the side of a building across the street. I couldn't plan that more perfectly if I did it myself. Everyone around me stopped to stare at the wreckage, giving me the opportunity to slip into the shadows. All the while, I hoped the people in the car and the building were okay.

I ducked into a breezeway and quickened my steps down the path into the forest. I had excellent sense of direction, plus my wolf helped. I just didn't see well at night.

Julie had all the connections set up for our scheme months before I agreed to fake my own death. Talk about premeditated.

Once I was out of sight from nosey human eyes, I created a small ball of light and directed it to float a couple of feet off the ground alongside me to light up my path. I had magic in my blood. Julie said it was like witch's magic but different, more powerful. I hadn't believed her at the time, which was about four years ago, shortly after we met. My mom wasn't a witch. Not that I know of, anyway.

Over the last few months, my powers had started to grow. So much that it was getting hard for me to hide the magic from my uncle and pack.

The rogue Alpha could never know about my power because he would use it for evil and to control me. Not happening.

Not today, Satan.

The growing magic in my veins was just another nail in my coffin. You know since I was going to die tonight. I had to leave the pack and death was the only way to do it.

I slowed my pace as the scent of old magic and burning wood reached my senses. I eased through the trees while keeping my senses open, cautious of my surroundings. Up ahead was a small cabin with smoke rolling from the chimney. That was the only sign that someone was inside the hovel of a home.

The wood slats on the outside looked weathered and need of replacing. Then again, it was most likely the magic surrounding the place that gave off the illusion of a rundown shack.

As I moved closer the front door opened and an old woman shorter than my five feet, two inches height filled the doorway. She had long white hair with wild corkscrew curls that seemed to have a mind of their own. Her wrinkled skin was pasty and as pale as a vampire's.

Please don't let her be some hybrid witch, vampire. She was scary enough.

"Are you going to stand out there all night?" The crone's voice was husky and cracked as she spoke, but the words held power and strength.

I stepped out of the tree line, inching closer to the old witch. Dark power flowed from her, making me uneasy. My wolf paced under my skin. Being unable to shift didn't mean that I couldn't feel my wolf. In fact, we had a strong bond and were almost perfectly in sync with each other.

If it wasn't for the fact that Julie trusted this woman and that I had to disappear fast, I wouldn't be here.

"A wolf with the powers of a sorceress. Interesting." The crone studied me for another few moments before turning to go back inside. "Come. We don't have all night."

Sorceress? Impossible. They were all hunted down and killed because they were too powerful. Since they were created by the Underworld gods, they were the darker version of witches. From what I heard sorceresses were as powerful as their godly creators, and just as deadly.

There was no way I was part sorceress. That would mean my father was one, since Mom was a wolf. Now that I thought about it, it would have been possible. I never knew my father. Mom said he died before I was born, and I had no reason to not believe her. Why would she lie to me? Especially about something like being a sorceress.

I came to abrupt stop, almost running into the witch. She whirled around and eyed me closely. Literally. She leaned in so close that all I saw were her strange, Champagne-colored eyes. Then she inhaled. Was she sniffing me? I hoped like hades I didn't stink. I hadn't showered that morning.

In a flash, she was gone, then reappeared on the other side of the room, in front of a closet. "Someone had bound your magic, but it isn't holding anymore."

She held up her hand with her palm up toward the ceiling. A small round bottle formed in her palm. "Come here."

I didn't like her tone. I also didn't understand what she was talking about. The magic in my veins was nothing like a sorceress's power. At least none that I heard anyway. Mine were weak in comparison.

Stepping closer to the old woman, I didn't take my eyes off her. She frowned and handed me the bottle in her hand. "Take this."

When I wrapped my hand around it, she grabbed my wrist, sending a jolt of panic through me. I tried to jerk free from her hold, but she was a lot stronger than she looked. She pulled me closer, making me stumble. "Do not open this bottle until you are ready to open your full powers. Whoever hid your magic, did it for a reason. However, I fear you will need your power sooner than later."

What the hell was she talking about?

Instead of explaining herself, she opened the closet, shoved me inside, and then slammed the door.

"Hey!" I pounded on the door just as purple smoke rose from the floor and a wave of dizziness came over me. *Oh, great. The crazy old hag gives me a potion to unlock my power then tries to kill me.*

"Let me out!" I pounded on the door again, ignoring the feeling of moving. It was like I was in a high-speed elevator.

The door opened and I tumbled out, falling on my face. I tightened my grip on the bottle, glad it didn't crash to the floor and break. The last thing I needed was to unlock my nonexistent sorceress's power. Knowing my luck there was an evil creature inside that bottle. Wait. That train of thought didn't help at all.

I glanced up at a tall slender man who had opened the door. He beamed down at me and flashed me a perfect smile. His blue eyes sparked with magic, and I instantly knew he was a witch. I'd always been able to tell what the different species were. Some it was their eyes and others it was their aura—the energy that surrounded them.

"Hi." I pushed myself to a stand and glanced around the room. It was an office. Was it his? "Where am I?"

I glanced back inside the closet and sure enough, it was just a closet. That old witch must had pushed me through a portal or something.

"Hex Towers." He held out his hand. "I'm Dylan Pearce, property manager." Then he pointed to the closet and added, "That is Hex Towers Portal One."

Portal one? The way he said it was like it was a secret or something. I took his hand and shook it, instantly feeling warmth coming from him. "Nice to meet you. I'm Mattie Carol."

He winked at me. "I know who you are, and it is a pleasure to finally meet you."

Finally? Was everyone going to be weird and cryptic?

Before I could respond, he opened his office door and ushered me out into a beautiful lobby fit for a palace. The smells of food and coffee invaded my senses and my stomach growled. My wolf pranced around, wanting me to scent every inch of the place. *Not now. We have plenty of time to get to know our new home.*

As we walked across the huge lobby, I couldn't help to take in the beauty of it. Crystal chandeliers hung in a row from one end to the other. A fountain set off to one side of the lobby. The center of it looked like a tree with a bat hanging upside down from one of the branches. The floor was pure white tiles, and I was betting they weren't cheap ceramic either. The walls were a cream color with burgundy trim and various accents with splashes of gold added in randomly throughout the space.

We stopped in front of the elevators and Dylan

turned to me, handing me a key card I hadn't seen him with earlier. Of course, he could have conjured it with magic. "This is the key to your apartment and to this elevator. You can't get to your floor without it."

That little tidbit helped me to relax. I had my own secure access. Or did I? "How many people are on my floor?"

"There are six apartments total on your floor, but this elevator only has access to two. It's very secure." The elevator opened and Dylan motioned me to go in first.

I couldn't help to wonder if Felix had anything to do with all the security. A feeling deep in my gut told me he did.

The ride to my floor, which was the second level from the top, was quick and smoother than I ever experience. We exited out into a small foyer with two doors in opposite corners. There were no numbers on them, which I found odd.

Dylan pointed to the door on the left, "That one is yours. Before you ask, no, we don't put numbers on the doors for security and privacy reasons for our residents."

Cool. It was a good thing that there were only two on my floor. Or I'd piss off a bunch of people for trying to get into their apartment because there was no way I'd remember where mine was without a number.

There wasn't a handle on the door, just a small black box to the right of it. I pressed the key card to the box and the lock clicked. Pushing the door open, I entered the apartment and my jaw dropped.

Dark hardwood floors stretched throughout the place, framed in with dark green floorboards. The walls were painted pale green. The living room was open to the kitchen, separated by a bar-style island. Directly across from the kitchen, on the other side of the living room, were two doors. I assumed that were the bedrooms.

Dylan moved to the floor to ceiling dark green curtains and opened them, spilling light into the room. I stopped next to Dylan and stared out the wall of glass. There was a balcony with seating and a small fire pit. Beyond that was a breathtaking view of Elliott Bay.

To keep my mind off faking my death, I did some research of Seattle and surrounding areas. I knew from the start that Felix would put us up in an apartment in the city. One that had tight security, like the one he lives in. I wouldn't be surprised if this was his building and he was the one to occupy the entire floor above the one I was on.

"Do you like it?" Dylan asked.

"Yes. It's gorgeous. Although I'm not sure how Julie and I can afford it." The rent on a place like this had to be more than my year's salary at the diner. And considering I didn't have a job at the moment, I definitely couldn't afford it.

Dylan snapped his fingers and an envelope appeared in his hand. "I almost forgot. This is for you. It's the paperwork for your records. And there is no rent because you own it."

Surly I was hearing things that weren't real. "How can I own? I never bought it."

Dylan smiled and took my hands. "Your mother did for when you were ready. That's why you are here."

"My mom?" My heart sank as I looked down at the envelop. "Why?"

Did Julie know? Did Felix? I was betting yes since he was in charge around here.

"Because she knew you would need it. But not until you were ready." Dylan glanced at his wrist as if he had a watch on, which he didn't. "Oh, look at the time. I have a meeting with the staff and managerial things to do." He kissed me on each cheek. "If you need anything at all, just call the front desk. They will know how to contact me."

Then he left.

I stood in front of the window for a little while longer before roaming around the large apartment. Seriously, it was huge compared to my tiny living space at the Claws Creek Pack den.

Once I picked my room, I set the envelop on the dresser, not opening it yet. I just knew seeing my mom's name and her signature would bring me to tears. It didn't matter that I was fourteen when she died and it's been, what, twenty-eight years since she left me in the care of my sadist uncle?

I didn't blame her for Roger. We had no other family, and she couldn't hide me from the mean-ass if she tried. Beside her death was sudden. There was no time to prep or hide. And up until she died, Roger wasn't too bad. At least I didn't think so. Then again, she could have been shielding me from him. The latter made sense to me.

The words from the old witch who shoved me into the closet portal floated around in my head. *Someone has bound your magic.*

I made my way to the kitchen and opened the cabinets, smiling when I discovered them packed with food and everything I need to cook and eat with. My wolf danced inside me at the notice of several of our favorite snacks. Turning to the fridge, I opened it and sighed at the various food items. My stomach reminded me it was there and still hungry.

Five minutes later, I had a large plate with a sandwich, cheese, and fruit, and I headed to the balcony. Once settled into one of the comfy chairs, I pulled out my phone and texted Julie. **Where are you? You never showed up for work. I'm worried. J.**

That was code since she had my phone and I had hers. Roger knew I had friends at work, although he never met Julie. So, my first message after I was safely in the apartment would be "Julie" worried because I never showed for work. That covered us for when someone found my phone at Reuben's house, where he supposedly would kill me tonight.

I searched through Julie's contacts and hovered my thumb over Felix's name. He was in Seattle somewhere and it would be nice to hear a familiar voice. But I couldn't call him from Julie's phone. I wasn't sure if he knew what our plan was.

What would he say? That we were crazy and putting ourselves at risk unnecessarily.

Whatever. I was free, or would be very soon, from Roger and the sadist he sold me to, and had a large expensive apartment in a city I was dying to explore.

Well, not dying...Okay so the pun was intended.

After I finished my lunch, I secured the glass door to the balcony, then stepped out of my apartment just my neighbor exited hers. She lifted her bright green gaze up to meet my stare and her face went from stoic to beautiful in seconds.

"Hi. You must be Matilda." She rushed forward and took my hand and shook it without me offering it. I had to suppress my urge to back away. She wouldn't be my neighbor if she intended to harm me. I had to believe that. These people were not like my pack.

Usually, I'd panic and run away from people when they got too close. Years of living in a pack full of rogues, made you have trust issues. However, there was something familiar about this woman. My wolf was leery, but she didn't snap at the female. My magic told me she could be trusted.

I am not weak!

My wolf repeated my words. *WE are not weak!*

"It's Mattie." I frowned. The only one who called me by my birth name was Felix. I figured it was a vampire thing and that he was older than God.

"Well, Mattie, it's great to meet you. I'm Anya."

She stepped back a little and tugged her blonde hair behind her ear. "Were you on your way out?"

"Yeah, I was going to see the city. I've never been here before."

Her smile brightened. "Would you like a guide?"

"That would be great."

CHAPTER TWO

My tour of downtown Seattle was amazing and disappointing. I forgotten that I needed an American ID and money. Then again, I hadn't planned on leaving my apartment until Julie got there. *Maybe I should call Felix.*

No. I would not call my BFF's ex beau and ask for money.

And I also wasn't going to let my new friend and neighbor, Anya, buy things for me. "I'll come back another day."

"I don't mind. And if you are worried about it, you can pay me back." Anya put the blouse back on the rack, then picked out something for herself.

Clothes weren't a big deal for me because I could conjure my own. At least for the time being. When I get a job and regular income flowing, I would be stocking my closet. I didn't know Anya well enough to trust her with my secrets just yet.

A few minutes later we were checking out of Nordstrom. Anya asked, "What do you want to do next?"

"I could go for an ice coffee." We'd been walking around for hours but it wasn't quite dinner time yet. Plus, I was addicted to sweets and coffee.

Anya's features brightened. "I know the perfect little locally owned coffee café. They have the best specialty drinks."

"Well, lead on."

The coffee café, aka Talon's Coffee House was a few blocks away. The mix of pastries and coffee flowed around me and was completely heaven. There was also an odd mix of spice notes that I haven't encountered before. It was alluring and warmed my insides.

We stepped up to the counter and I froze as I stared into a sea of blue irises. Holy crap, what beautiful eyes he had. Blinking, I roamed my gaze over the rest of his face and down his chest. Too bad below the waist was hidden by the counter he stood behind.

My wolf growled softly before saying, *mine.*

Yes, that would be nice. Wait? *He's our mate?*

Yep.

Oh, no. The last thing I needed was a mate.

Anya nudged me, drawing me from talking to my wolf, and said, "This is Talon."

As in Talon's Coffee House. Oh, great, I was ogling the owner. Openly.

Talon held out his hand and smiled. The curve of his lips sent a hot shiver through my body and I almost fell out on the floor because my legs were suddenly unsteady. "Hello and welcome to Seattle."

I glanced at his hand, and then back up to his face. Big mistake. My wolf was pacing, wanting to rub all over this man, whom was not a wolf. Talon was a witch. I sensed his magic flowing around him.

Snapping out of my embarrassing trance, I shook his hand and forced a smile. Well, I didn't have to actually force my smile because he was so easy on the eyes. And I was a free woman. No Roger or pack-mates to tell me I was worthless. "It is that obvious that I'm new here?"

Something passed over his features but was gone in a flash as he pointed to Anya. "I know all her friends, which isn't many, but I don't know you, so I assumed you are new to town."

Sounded legit. "You guessed right."

I studied his handsome features. Square jaw. A nose that was slightly crooked but only added to his rugged sexiness.

"She's my new neighbor," Anya added, then gave her order.

Talon punched in Anya order and lifted his gaze to mine. "Welcome to Hex Towers."

"Thank you." I gave my order, and Anya and I took a seat by the window.

After a few minutes of silence, I asked, "So Talon lives in Hex Towers?"

Anya nodded. "Yeah. He and I are like brother and sister. We've known each other forever. At least it seems that way."

Good to know. No, it wasn't. Now I was going to hang out in the lobby trying to accidently run into him daily. Could I be more pathetic?

I really couldn't, especially since Talon was a possible mate for me. That was the last thing I needed. So I had to make sure to keep Talon at a distance. There was no need to get him caught up in my mess of a past. Namely my uncle, the bastard rogue alpha.

"I think he likes you. I haven't seen him this interested in another person in a long time." Anya paused as Talon came over to deliver our drinks. "Talon, when do you get off?"

My mind went three hundred shades of dirty with Anya's last statement. I was so not going there.

It'd been a very long time since I dated. No one in the pack would give me the time of day because they thought I was the omega. No wolf wanted a weak female.

"I can leave any time. I'm the owner."

Anya rolled her eyes. "Smart ass." Then she looked at me. "We could have dinner together. My place or yours? I'll cook either way."

Um, what choice did I have. If I said no, it would be rude. Plus, I liked Anya. There was something about her that made me feel secure and at ease. It was the same when Julie and I first met. I've learned in my forty-five years of life to trust my instincts. "Sure. We can hang at my place."

And just like that, I had Mr. Coffee Hottie coming over for dinner. At least I wouldn't be alone with him.

"Great, I'll see you two ladies in about an hour." Talon made eye contact with me and my insides danced with excitement as did my wolf. Then he left to go back to work.

Anya laughed and stood, picking up her drink. "He is totally into you."

"I have too much baggage to entertain the idea of dating right now." I didn't mean to say that out loud. Oops.

To my relief, Anya didn't ask me to explain. Instead, she said, "We all have baggage."

True, but my baggage could get people killed. I kept that to myself. At least I hoped I did.

On our way back to Hex Tower, I spotted an art store. I loved to paint and draw and couldn't resist the urge to go inside. It was a good thing that Anya didn't mind.

As soon as I entered the store, I felt the tingles of magic flowing in the air. It was calming and liberating at the same time. A powerful witch owned the store, I was sure of it based on the energy that nipped at my skin.

I moved through the aisles taking in the diverse selection of paints, brushes, and canvases. There were even finished painting displayed throughout the store. My creative side raged to life and my fingers itched to grab the supplies I needed to start painting again. Something I hadn't done since Mom died.

Grabbing my wallet from inside my bag, I

checked my cash. I've never had credit cards. Roger didn't like them because you could be tracked by your spending. My evil uncle also didn't like technology for the same reason. I guess when you run from the law as for as long as he had, you got paranoid.

I had two hundred dollars, but I needed to make it stretch until I got a job. However, I didn't have to pay rent and the pantry and refrigerator were stocked with food. I could pick up something small.

Picking out a sketch book and colored pencils, I took my loot to the counter where Anya was waiting for me. She was texting on her phone with her brows drawn together and her mouth pursed.

"That's a serious text."

She jerked her head up and instantly relaxed. "Sorry, was I making a face? I do that when talking to the boss."

"I know the feeling." Only I made my faces at Roger. I set my loot on the counter. "Where do you work?"

For a brief second, Anya stilled. If I hadn't spent my life noticing every movement, expression, and scent change from my uncle, I would have missed Anya's little reactions to my questions. She'd been doing it all day. It was enough to make me reconsider trusting her.

At least, I was that desperate for friends that I was willing to risk it. Plus, I felt her energy, it was laced with good intentions. Just like Hell was paved with it.

"Private security. My boss is a stubborn SOB." Anya grinned at me as she slid her phone in her back pocket. "Is that all you are getting?"

I pushed the sketch book and pencils to the cashier, who was exotically beautiful. Her eyes were a mix of Asian descent and otherworldly. Her skin was the color of light honey and seemed to glow. It was her hair that I was envious of. The coloring resembled a raven's wing—black with purples and blues visible when the light hit it just right.

The cashier smiled at me. "Who have you brought in today, Anya?"

Glancing at Anya, I noticed that she didn't seem to want to answer the cashier. "This is Matilda. She is my new neighbor."

"I see," The cashier said, focusing back on me. "New recruit?"

Confused, I watched Anya work her jaw. She clearly either didn't like this woman or didn't want to share me with her. Which could be the same thing.

Anya's phone chimed from her back pocket and rolled her eyes before answering the woman's question. "No. Mattie is a friend."

Having about enough of the weird exchange between the two, I held out my hand to the cashier. "Nice to meet you."

Before the other woman had a chance to shake my hand, Anya leapt forward and moved my hand away. "Don't let people in this town that you don't know touch you."

I stared at Anya like she lost her mind because I had no idea what she was talking about. If sensing, my further confusion, Anya said, "This is Tania. She owns the store, and she is a fae with psychic abilities. She can read people and things by touch. Their past, present, and future. And she is nosey."

Tania shrugged, her lips curving in a grin. "Guilty. I like to know who comes in my store." She held up the sketch book. "Mattie is more than she seems."

Crap. Tania read something from the book since I just held it in my hand. But what did she see?

There must had been panic written all over my face, because Tania frowned and placed my art supplies in a bag and handed it to me. "I hadn't intended to read you as Miss High and Mighty said. I don't do it unless asked to."

I took the bag and pulled out my wallet from my tote. Tania shook her head. "That's on the house. I have a feeling you'll be shopping here often."

Yes, I would as soon as I got a handle on my finances. Like get some finances to handle.

"Thank you."

I barely got the words out of my mouth as Anya pulled me out of the store. "She's so nosey."

"She seems nice."

Anya snorted. "Yeah, until she steals your heart and breaks it into a million pieces."

CHAPTER THREE

"You and Tania dated?" I asked after the elevator doors closed. I didn't mean for my question to come out as surprised as it sounded.

Anya let out a breathy laugh. "For about a year. It was complicated. And a long time ago."

The way Anya refused to look at me as she spoke, told me that she really didn't want to talk about it. I got the feeling she wasn't over the art store owner.

"I didn't mean to sound shocked or judgey. I just don't get out much." Wow, did I just say that? Gods, could I sound more juvenile?

Relief flooded me when Anya didn't ask me to elaborate. I didn't need my new friends to know just how sheltered my life had been.

When we exited the elevator, Anya moved toward her apartment. "I'm going to grab some wine. Do you like white or red?"

Pressing my lips together, I frowned. "I'm not sure. I had some at a mating ceremony once that I didn't like."

"That was probably cheap shit, or something. You might not be a wine person." Anya unlocked her door. "I'll grab a few bottles and we'll do wine tasting."

"Sounds fun." I didn't have the heart to tell her I had never drank before except that one time I tried that glass of wine at the mating ceremony. That was a few years ago.

My taste could have changed. Maybe it was the brand of wine or whatever I didn't like. I had no clue because I didn't know anything about it.

As soon as I entered my apartment my cell rang. I dug it out of my pocket and set my bag from the art store down on the coffee table. My pulse jumped when I saw my own name flash on the screen. "Hi Julie!"

"You sound great for a dead person."

I laughed and sank into the comfy leather sofa. "I feel pretty good too."

"I'm on my way to the witch's house to take the

portal express. I should be there in a few hours." Julie fell silent for a few heart beats. "Your sorry ass uncle isn't even throwing you a memorial."

That was not a shock to me. "Did you expect him to?"

"I guess not. But he surprised me by going to Ruben's house when you didn't show up when he expected you to. I thought he wouldn't look for you for a few days." Julie's tone turned serious as she continued. "Was he always like that? Kept you on a short leash? No pun intended."

I couldn't help but laugh. "It's sad but true. Now you understand why at forty-five years old I haven't experienced things that most my age has. It's pretty pathetic. What happened?"

"Roger showed about an hour ago. Believe me, not breathing and pretending to be dead for five hours is harder than it sounded." Julie laughed. "At first Roger freaked out. He cursed you for an hour for being weak, by the way."

I snorted and conjured my blue tooth earpiece so I can listen to her and check out my new art supplies. "I bet. Ruben hates weak females, so I pretended to be one as much as possible hoping he'd tell Roger to pick someone else."

I feared one of the reasons why Ruben put up

with my attempts to be everything he didn't want in a female was my magic. And the fact that I was an alpha. There were a few times I let it slip through my mental shields. Another reason why he wanted me more was it was too hard to keep my attitude contained as well. The man pissed me off by breathing.

Ruben saw my spark and fire of a personality even though he never called me out on it. I figured he was plotting to beat it out of me once I moved in with him. Hence the reason I needed an out. AKA my untimely, premeditated death.

"I'm not sure he can pick anyone else now."

"What do you mean?"

"Ruben had his guys wrap me up in the rug I bled all over, so I didn't see much. Then they carried me out of the house. That made hearing what went on between him and Roger was no go. I guessed I was in the backyard, but I knew I was outside because I smelled the earth and heard birds." Julie paused and it sounded like she covered the phone with her hand. I could hear her placing a food order.

I almost told her that we were eating around the time she got here, but knowing Julie, she'd eat again. She ate all the time, and I never knew where she put it all.

"Anyway, where was I? Oh, yeah outside, birds, the smell of earth. I heard a car in the distance then the slamming of doors like a bunch of people climbing out. At least that was the image that popped in my mind. Then I heard your uncle barking orders. Yes, he was actually barking. He was so pissed, and I swore I heard fear in his tone. But not like he was afraid for his own life."

What? Was he concerned that Ruben hurt me or killed me? My uncle didn't care for anyone else but himself. Why would he fear for my life? Of course, the point of Julie framing Ruben was to make sure my uncle wouldn't search for me.

Gods, I hope this worked.

Julie continued. "I'm not sure what happened. There was a lot of yelling and it sounded like a fight broke out inside the house. I waited until everything fell silent and the car drove off before I unwrapped myself from the rug. When I got inside, the house was destroyed, and Ruben was nowhere to be found. All his men were dead."

My stomach dropped to my feet and my head began to pound. What have I done? "Do you think Roger killed Ruben?" But why?

"Yeah. The emotional signature left behind in the house was rage and pain. I think your uncle cared for you in his own sick, twisted way. The thought that you were dead, drove him to murder." Julie's voice started to break up like she was in an area with bad cell service.

Before I could think too much on my uncle's reaction to my death, a knock sounded on my door. I picked up the phone and carried it to see who it was. A quick looksee in the peep hole, showed Anya's beautiful face. I opened the door and smiled.

Anya held up two bottles of wine in one hand as she gripped the necks between her fingers, and a bottle of whiskey in the other. Ah, it was nice to have options. "I thought I'd bring a backup in case you didn't like the wine."

"Thanks,"

"Who is that?" Julie asked in my ear. Not that she was actually in my ear. She spoke through the Bluetooth earpiece.

I pointed to the device in my ear so Anya would know I was talking on the phone while I answered Julie's question. "Our neighbor, Anya. We went exploring the city today."

Julie was silent for several seconds. "You shouldn't be exploring until we know for sure you weren't followed."

"Could people follow a portal?"

"Some can trace the magic used to create the portal."

I didn't know that. "But this is my uncle we're talking about. I'm sure there aren't many who like him enough to do something like that."

I tried to keep my end of the conversation as innocent as possible for Anya's sake. I didn't want her to think I was a rogue or something.

"Who is this, Anya?" Julie asked, possessiveness in her tone.

I studied my neighbor and decided to describe her to Julie. "She has long blonde hair that looks like spun gold, bright green eyes, and is taller than me."

"Everyone is taller than you."

"Ha. Ha." I crinkled my nose and met Anya's curious gaze.

With a sideways grin, Anya asked, "Are you signing me up for a dating site? If so, don't bother. I'm done with relationships."

"Oh, that Anya." Julie laughed. "Did she tell you what she does for a living?"

"She said personal security."

Anya frowned and mouthed, "who is that?"

I mouthed, "Julie."

Then my bestie spoke in my ear again. "Well,

that's true. In a way. She is one of Felix's personal guards. Apparently, she's yours now if she is there."

"But she's not a vampire."

Anya gave me a look of shock, then just as fast she rolled her eyes and said, "Oh, that Julie."

My best friend heard Anya and chuckled. "I have to go now. I'm at the old witch's house." She paused and cursed. "Felix just texted and wants me to pick up something for him."

"How does he know you have my phone?"

"I told him the plan. I had to because he's a nosey bugger. Besides he needed to know all the details to provide you with the protection you need. I'll see you in the morning." Julie didn't give me a chance to say bye. She never like saying it so it didn't bother me.

Knowing that she would be here in the morning made me relax. I hadn't realized just how worried I'd been about Julie until that moment.

Setting my, well Julie's phone, on the counter, I met Anya's stare and smirked. "So, you know Julie and you're one of Felix's enforcers or whatever he calls you."

Anya shrugged and uncorked a bottle of red wine. "Guilty."

I studied her for a moment and decided not to

give her a hard time about lying to me. Then again, she didn't actually lie. She omitted the truth. That's kind of the same thing but whatever. I had no doubt that she was under Felix's orders to keep me in the dark.

Anya handed me the glass of wine. I took a sip. Fruit notes with a spice on the backend burst to life in my mouth. "Hey this is good."

"I thought you might like that one. It's one of my favorites." When a knock sounded on the door, I moved to answer it, but Anya beat me to it. "No one should be able to get up here without either of us knowing it."

She opened the door and frowned at Talon. "How did you get up here?"

He grinned and pushed passed her to enter my apartment. "I've been invited. Plus, I still have your spare key."

Shutting the door, Anya glared at Talon. "It's supposed to be used for emergencies."

"This is. I had to get up here before you attempted to cook dinner." Talon flashed me a smiled that made my insides tingle.

He was good looking, and he could cook. I moved around him and the island that separated the living room from the kitchen. "What makes you think I can't cook," I teased as I searched the fridge for our options.

When I turned, I crashed into a wall of muscle. Talon's hands rested on my hips and heat flooded me. His scent enveloped me in a sensual embrace, drawing me closer. One side of his mouth lifted in a half smile, forming a dimple. "Can you cook?"

I stared into his blue eyes and completely forgot his question. "What?"

He chuckled and stepped back. Instantly I missed the feel of his hands on me. "Can you cook," he repeated.

"Yes." Giving him my back, I caught Anya sitting on a bar stool on the other side of the island, watching us with interest. I ignored her and focused on dinner. When I pulled out a package of meat, wrapped in white paper, Talon took it from me and pushed me toward Anya. "Let me. You drink your wine and relax."

I sat on the stool next to Anya. Who was I to tell the gorgeous man no? If he wanted to cook me dinner, then he was welcome to it. Besides, I'd never had a male do things for me. Life in the Claws Creek Pack was fend for yourself or die. Males in my pack didn't care for their mates like they should. Then again, I wasn't sure that those who had mates were truly bonded.

A true bond was strong and if you hurt your mate, you hurt yourself because you felt each other's pain, happiness, and all other emotions. Or so I was told.

I wouldn't know. I'd never been lucky enough to find my mate. Until now. And I wasn't sure what to do about it.

CHAPTER FOUR

It was late afternoon before I woke. In my defense, I didn't crash until four in the morning. My new neighbors helped me polish off both bottles of wine and the whiskey. Well, Anya did. Talon didn't drink, which added to his appeal. Not because I was a hypocrite. I wasn't. I didn't drink often, and I had never been as shitfaced as I was last night.

I never felt safe enough to drink that much nor sleep in as late as I had with other people in the apartment. Two people. Strangers, yet they seemed familiar in a déjà vu kind of way. The universe was telling me that I was on the right path.

Gods, I hope so.

Glancing down at myself, because I couldn't remember if I changed out of my clothes last night before passing out on top of my covers. It was a good thing wolves ran hot. Even half breeds like myself. Plus, I was full on with perimenopause, meaning hot flashes that weren't flashes at all.

I was wearing my black boy shorts with the tiny red lips in a repeat pattern and a black tank top. Good enough. All the important bits were covered, not that nudity bothered me anyway since I was raised in a wolf pack. Shifters were comfortable in their birthday suits.

When I exited my bedroom to the living room, I spotted Anya sitting in one of the overstuffed chairs with her phone in hand. Stopping in front of her, I watched her for a few moments. Her blonde hair spilled over her shoulder and was still damp from a shower. "Afternoon. Did you stay here all morning?"

Anya looked up from her phone and smirked. "I slept for a few hours and then went to my place to shower and check in with Felix. She nodded to Talon, who was asleep on the couch, and rolled her eyes. "He wouldn't leave until he was sure you woke up alive. We did have a lot to drink last night."

Yeah, and I was sure I would never drink like that again. Although I didn't have a hangover, which was a good thing.

"Really?" I studied the sleeping Talon as another

piece of the wall I kept around my heart crumbled. I'd never had anyone care about my wellbeing since my mom died. "Is he one of my protectors?"

There had to be a reason why, Talon, a stranger to me, would feel the need to make sure I didn't die of alcohol poisoning. Although as far as I knew I couldn't. It took a lot to get a shifter drunk, but I wasn't full shifter.

"No. He doesn't work for Felix." Anya set her phone on the arm of the chair and stood. "How are you feeling?"

"Fine. A little lazy and total lack of motivation, but fine." In fact, besides being a little anxious about being on my own, I felt great.

Glancing around, I had the strange feeling something was missing. Then it hit me. Not something, someone. Julie. "Did Julie make it in this morning?"

Anya frowned. "I haven't seen her."

Dread settled in the pit of my stomach. Maybe that was the alcohol from the night before. Either way, it wasn't like Julie to not show up when she said she would. Or at least call me to let me know what was up.

"I'm sure she'll show." Anya pulled out her phone and typed on it.

"She said that Felix wanted her to pick up something, then she was coming straight here." I darted back into my room and grabbed the cell phone, checking for messages. There were none.

Damn.

I called Julie and waited. About the tenth or so ring, I glanced up when Anya appeared in the doorway. Shaking my head, I said, "She's not answering."

Panic burned my insides and my wolf whimpered. What if Roger found out what we did? And he had Julie killed.

Anya crossed the room and gripped my upper arms, forcing me to lock gazes with her. "Julie is strong and pretty hard to kill."

She was right. Julie was also smart and resourceful. My best friend was fine. I was being paranoid. "Still, it isn't like her to not call."

Talon suddenly appeared at my bedroom door. "What's wrong?"

For a moment I forgot how to speak and breathe. The sight of him did things to my body that were foreign to me. I'd never had a response to anyone like when I looked at Talon. Don't get me started on how delicious he smelled. His brown hair was chaos of waves on the top of his head, enhancing the sex in sexy.

Mine.

The word echoed in my head, startling me out of the lovesick trance this male put me in. I was so not ready to go down the mating road.

Nope. Not when I was desperately trying to find my independence and break from my uncle's control.

And that was another thing. Would he want me after finding out I was on the run from a rogue pack? And that I was the Alpha's niece? And the pack omega?

There was only one way to find out. Just rip that bandage off. It was better to find out now than later when his rejection would hurt far more. Besides, I thought Anya already knew most of my story since she worked for Felix.

With a sigh, I sat on my bed and pulled a pillow into my lap, hugging it to my body. "Julie and I faked my death."

Anya's features didn't change, which confirmed that she knew. Talon, however, narrowed his gaze and folded his arms over his broad chest. "Why?"

"Because my bastard of an uncle sold me to an Alpha who is cruel and notorious for killing his mates in violent fits of rage." A shudder went through me so hard it was impossible for me to keep them from noticing. Saying the words out loud made my stomach roll. But I was free from Ruben. "My pack is not a nice one, but my betrothed makes them look like angels of mercy."

Before Talon could say anything, I spilled all my demons—my heartless uncle, my struggle with hiding the growing powers from my witch half, and my need for a fresh start. When I finished, tears streamed down my face and Talon had me cradled in his lap, rocking me while running his fingers through my hair.

He kissed my forehead and said, "I wondered why Anya acted weird when I asked about you."

I lifted my head and glared at him. "When did you ask about me?"

He chuckled. "Last night when you passed out."

Embarrassment colored my cheek. "I don't drink, usually."

He pressed a finger to my lips and grinned at me. "Don't make excuses. Besides it sounds like you needed last night."

I really did.

"I fear that Roger found out that Julie pretended to be me and killed her."

Talon tightened his arms around me. "Julie is a fae and pretty hard to kill."

I studied him for a long while. As I opened my

mouth to speak a knock sounded on the apartment door. Who the hell could that be?

Anya exited the bedroom to answer it. I shared a look with Talon before we followed her. She opened the door and Felix walked in.

"Felix." I rushed to him and threw my arms around him. My head came to the center of his chest. "Please tell me you heard from Julie."

"I have not." He lifted my chin to look into my eyes. "Tell me what she said when you last spoke."

I told him and he directed me to the couch. Talon hovered close, glaring at Felix. I didn't even have the energy for male egos, so I ignored it. For now.

"I had her do a job before she was to come here. When the object I requested appeared in my study, I figured she was here and just avoiding me." Felix's featured took on harsh lines and angles as he thought about the situation. He moved his dark gaze to me and asked, "She hadn't shown up at all?"

"No. I tried calling but she didn't answer." Fear that I caused Julie's death spread through me like a wildfire.

Talon picked up his phone from the coffee table and started typing on it as he sat on the other side of me. "My brother is the Seattle Police Chief. I am sending him a text to let me know if he runs across anyone matching Julie's description. What does she look like?"

Before I could answer, Felix described Julie like he was having a painting of her commissioned. As Felix spoke, Talon typed. When he was done, Anya said, "I'll call hospitals in and around Seattle and in Canada."

Felix took my hands in his and gave a gentle squeeze. "I'll send a team out to search for her. We will find her."

There was no doubt in his words, and it made me feel a little better. I still worried that Roger had found out about our plan. If he hadn't, would he find out eventually? I needed to be prepared if that happened.

"Felix, I need to learn to defend myself and to control my magic. I feel it growing stronger."

The ancient vampire nodded once then gestured to Talon. "He will see to your magic and Anya and Julie will work with you to build your strength. You will also join the enforcer training a few times a week."

Felix stood and moved to the door where he looked at me over his shoulder and said, "Welcome home, Matilda."

CHAPTER FIVE

I'd spent the rest of the day organizing and decorating the apartment, making it more like me. Plus, I needed something to keep my mind from worrying about Julie. It didn't matter that my best friend was a powerful fae, she could survive anything.

The latter is something I repeated to myself several times throughout the day. Decorating the apartment also helped and it felt amazing to be able to make every inch of the place mine. When we find Julie and she comes home, she'll add her personal touches to the place.

We'll make it our home where I'm free from everything I was running from.

Opening the closet door in my bedroom, I

studied the contents inside. Or the lack of stuff I owned. I'd never seen a closet that big before. It was like a third bedroom. And it was perfect for storing my art supplies.

I set to work on getting the oversized closet cleaned out. Talon should be returning soon with the items I asked him to pick up from the hardware store when he got off work.

When I lived with my uncle, I spent my time organizing and cleaning. It helped to calm me, so I didn't expose the magic I had. The same magic that seemed to be growing stronger.

At the back of the closet was an old trunk. I moved closer and frowned when I tried to open it and found it was locked. A hum of magic surrounded the trunk. Odd.

I hovered my hand over the top of the trunk then moved down both sides and around the back of it. All along feeling the magic pulsing from it.

Sitting on the floor in front of locked chest, I tilted my head while glaring at the thing.

Use your magic, my wolf said as she pushed forward as if wanting a closer look at the thing.

"I don't know how to use my magic." A frowned formed, bring an ache to my chest. I never had anyone to help me with my magic. Roger sure didn't take any interest in training me. My theory on that was he was afraid I'd be more powerful than he was.

Then again, he didn't like witches much. Mom told me when I was small it was best that I never showed him just how powerful I could be.

There's only one way to learn.

I rolled my eyes at my wolfs words. "I'd say the same about you and the not wanting to shift thing."

Her reply was a huff that sounded like a sneeze. She had never admitted that she didn't want to shift. I assumed it was because I was part human and the fact that she hated Roger and the other males in the pack.

My keen wolf hearing heard the bell on the elevator ding followed by footsteps in the small foyer that Anya and I shared. It sounded like Anya, but I couldn't be certain because I haven't been around my new friends long enough to recognize them by the way they walk.

After pushing to a stand, I picked up the chest and carried it into the living room where I placed it on the coffee table just as a knock sounded on the door.

The scent of rosemary and sage reached my nose and I smiled. Anya. I opened the door and cocked an eyebrow. She was loaded down with bags from several different stores. I took a few from her and led the way to the sofa. "What is all this?"

I had asked her to go Tania's art store and pick up a few canvases and brushes. This was a lot more than that unless she figured I needed a sofa full of art supplies.

Anya shrugged. "I picked up a few items to do a tracking spell. Plus a few extras."

That was more than a few extras. But the tracking spell sounded interesting. "Can you teach me to do spells?"

Anya studied me for a few moments. "No one taught you to use magic?"

I shook my head as I opened one of the bags. "My mom died before my powers made an appearance. My uncle hated magic, so I never told him about mine."

"Really? How old were you when your mom died?"

"Fourteen." I pulled a few canvases out of the larger bag and looked over at Anya. "How much did Felix tell you about me?"

Picking up all the bags with a pentagram on them, Anya carried them into the kitchen. I followed as she replied to my question. "Not much, just that you are family and need to be protected. And that your uncle is an evil shithead."

A snort escaped from me, making Anya laugh which only made me laugh more. "Shithead is too nice of a word for Roger."

"Yeah, I gathered that when you said you had to fake your death to get away." Anya pulled out a mirror out of one of the bags that could double as a pizza pan. The edges of the mirror had symbols etched into the glass.

"What's that? Besides a mirror."

Anya tapped the center of the mirror and magic rippled across the surface. "This is my scrying mirror. One of my talents is to find lost or misplaced things."

"Oh cool." I pulled up a barstool and sat while watching her set up for the tracking spell. "Will you teach me magic?"

"Of course. Talon will help too. His power is different from mine."

I was about to ask how different when a single knock sound on the door before it opened. Talon's woodsy scent filled my apartment and I had to force myself not to sniff the air. I didn't need him to think I was weird or anything.

Turning on my stool, I gave him a smile. "Anya and you will be teaching me magic."

A spark lit up his eyes as he locked gazes with me and crossed the room. He opened the bag he was carrying to reveal the nails, hammer, and a few other things I requested from the hardware store. When I started to take the bag from him, he moved it away. "I'll do it, just tell me what you want hung and where."

He's a keeper, my wolf said with a seductive growl.

Calm down. The last thing we need is to be controlled by another male. As soon as the thought was sent to my wolf, I knew I was being paranoid. I didn't sense anything from Talon that told me he was anything like the males from the pack.

One thing was for sure, I didn't want to rush into a relationship. Mate or not. Plus, I didn't know how to tell him that he was mine.

"Hey," Talon said and touched my cheek. "What's wrong?"

He pulled his hand back too fast, so I grabbed it and held on to it. "Nothing, just thinking and talking to my wolf. She talks to me a lot, so if I'm acting like an insane person, ignore me."

He chuckled and dang if the sound didn't vibrate all the way to my soul.

Make him laugh again.

Ignoring my wolf, I focused on Talon. "I'm perfectly capable of hanging my own pictures and art."

He stared at me for a long moment and twisted his hand so our fingers linked together. At the same time, he sat the bag on a nearby end table. "I know you can do it. I wasn't implying that you couldn't."

I cringed, realizing that my words were a little too defensive. Years of pretending to be an omega formed habits that I didn't like, but it was what I had to do to survive in a pack full of rogue wolves.

But I wasn't in that pack anymore and I needed to find my independence. I didn't have to pretend anymore. That didn't mean I had to snap at my soon-to-be mate. "I'm sorry I snapped."

He stepped closer to me and with his free hand, ran his knuckles down my cheek. I released a soft sigh and leaned into his touch. Then he said, "Don't ever apologize to me. I would like to help if you let me."

If I let him...

Those simple words touched me much deeper

than I thought possible. No one had ever said those things to me. "Of course, you can help."

"I hate to interrupt because it looks like you two are having a moment, but I'm ready to do the spell," Anya interrupted.

The spell. Julie.

Crap. I lost focus, again. Slipping my hands from Talon's, I turned to Anya. Her amused smirk made me flush. I hadn't realized until then just how much I wanted Talon. The mating pull was a powerful thing.

"I'm ready." I grinned at her as I sat back on the stool. "What do I need to do?"

Anya had set the island countertop up like an altar. Lavender was scattered around the mirror and a single white candle was lit. The soft scent of frankincense filled the air along with a spark of magic. Anya's magic.

"I've never felt your magic until now."

She shrugged. "I keep it hidden from others. It makes my job easier if people believed I'm human."

That was true. And now I was wondering what type of jobs she did for Felix. Then again, I might be better off not knowing. I'll definitely ask Julie about it.

Anya pointed to the top corner of mirror closest

to me. "Place your hand there and visualize Julie. See her in your mind, then I'll do my thing."

As soon as my palm touched the mirror, it warmed. I took a breath and closed my eyes and instantly recalled Julie's face. I pictured her from the last time I saw her. It was in that diner.

I felt the moment Anya touched the mirror and again when she pushed her power into the glass. Then everything stopped. The mirror cooled instantly.

Opening my eyes, I glanced down and frowned. "What happened?"

"Nothing," Anya said. "I'm not sure what happened, other than it didn't work."

I didn't know jack about magic, so I wasn't sure what to say. Thankfully, Talon did. "Do you think she's being blocked?"

Anya shrugged. "It's possible. I'm sorry, Mattie, I thought we'd get a location and go kick some ass and bring her home."

"It's not your fault. We'll find her another way." I wasn't sure what that would be at the moment, but there had to be another way.

Just then Talon's phone let off a series of beeps. He pulled it from his back pocket, glanced at it, then answered. "Sup."

My wolf hearing allowed me to hear the man on the other end of the call. "A car matching the description you gave me earlier was found on I4 about a mile outside of city limits."

"Just the car?" Talon's features turned serious and sad.

My chest tightened and I fought to breathe. What if Julie was dead? As soon as the question formed in my head, Talon reached out and took my hand. Instantly, I calmed.

"Thanks," Talon hung up and slipped his phone into his back pocket. "I take it you heard." I nodded and he gave my hand a gentle squeeze. Then told Anya what the man on the phone said. "That was River, and he said a car matching Julie's was found and it's being towed to Mac's."

A smile lifted Anya's lips. "I want to go see if we can get anything that would help the tracking spell work."

Oh, that sounded fun. "Count me in!"

Talon held up a finger and at first, I thought he was going to tell me to sit this one out. Instead, he said, "First, I'll cook dinner. It's best we wait until nightfall since we'll be breaking into the impound yard."

"That sounds like a plan."

CHAPTER SIX

Talon lent me one of his navy blue hoodies and it fell to about mid-thigh. It went perfect with my dark blue skinny jeans. "You sure it's not too big?"

I could conjure my own that fit a little better, but having his scent wrapped around me made my insides heat up.

Anya shook her head. "No, it's perfect. You look like one of the street kids that hang out in that area."

"I'm not sure that is a good idea." Worry replaced my desire for Talon. But only a little.

Talon chuckled. "What she means is that you will blend in and if the cameras catch us, which I'm hoping not, the police will think it was kids breaking in."

Ah, that made sense. And it was smart thinking. "I'm ready then."

"Let's roll," Talon said with a wink and took the lead out of my apartment.

Talon drove through downtown and out to a small neighborhood that was a mix of industrial and residential. He parked about a block from the impound yard. We walked through a couple adjacent properties to reach the back of what looked like a junk yard with a chain linked fence surrounding it. A small trailer-like building sat at one end of the yard.

I searched the rows of cars but couldn't see much because the sun had set by the time we got there. Even though I was a wolf shifter, I didn't have supernatural night vision. Another reason why I was the omega of my old pack.

Anya quickly climbed over the fence and dropped soundlessly on the other side. She made it look so easy. I loved climbing trees when I was younger. Climbing a fence shouldn't be much harder, right?

I got to the top and tried to mimic Anya's movements as I threw myself over the top. Only I didn't land like Anya did. The hoodie I wore got hooked on the top of the chain-link fence, causing me to slam into it, announcing our presence.

Damn. I held my breath, waiting for light to turn on or a snarling dog to charge at us. Neither of those things happened, which I was relieved. Talon came to my rescue and unhooked the hoodie from the fence, then carried me down the other side.

"Thanks." I kept my voice low and my senses sharp. It bothered me that no one heard the fence rattle. I picked up a scent that wasn't human. "There are dogs here. Why hadn't they come running when I hit the fence?"

Talon gave me a crooked grin. "I created a bubble around us as soon as you reached to top. Just in case."

"I'm not as coordinated as I was when I was younger." I left it at that and followed Anya to search for Julie's car.

"Do you see it?" Talon whispered in my ear as we made our way down the second row of cars.

I frowned and shook my head. "I can't see in the dark."

"But you are a wolf," he replied a little louder as if shocked by the news.

I shrugged and met Anya's gaze as she turned to look at me. "I can't shift either. That's why I was the omega of the pack and my uncle thought I would be better off mated to a sadist."

Talon stopped, making me do the same and face him. His features were a mix of anger and confusion. "One." He held up a finger. "You are not an omega. "Two, you are only half wolf, which still doesn't make you an omega."

I waved him off and started walking again. "I'm not one anymore. My pack believes I'm dead."

My pack status was in the past. That was where I wanted it to stay. Apparently, Talon wasn't going to let it go. "We will talk about that later. Right now, we need to find Julie's car before we are caught."

I wasn't looking forward to that conversation. "What about the dogs I smelled near the fence?"

Anya answered me with a wink. "I took care of them."

"Please tell me you didn't hurt them."

"Of course not. They are distracted with some treats, but that won't last for long, so we do need to hurry." She turned and moved between two cars to the next row over.

I followed and a few feet down the aisle, I spotted Julie's car. "There it is."

We rushed over to the car and Anya pulled a small box from her hoodie pocket. Inside were some ritual items and little potion bottles. She pulled one of the bottles out and opened it before speaking a chant in Latin. Burnt orange colored smoke rose out of the bottle and surrounded the car. Once it fully covered the vehicle, the smoke changed to a deep purple, then disappeared back inside the bottle.

"Is that it?" I've never seen anything like it. Of course, I hadn't because I didn't know any witches. Julie was the only person I knew that had magic in her veins like me.

Anya nodded. "The first part. Then next part I can do at your place. The spell will need time to cook, for lack of a better way to explain it. You can go through the car now if you need to get anything of hers out of there. I'm sure Felix will have it towed to the Hex Towers garage, but it's better that we go through it first."

I couldn't agree more.

Opening the driver door, I was hit with two scents at once. One of the scents belonged to Julie and I was betting the other was from her kidnapper. I refused to believe she was anything but alive.

"The kidnapper is a human male." I reached in and grabbed Julie's backpack that sat on the passenger seat, then dug around in the console between the seats. My phone was in there, which I found odd. I grabbed it and checked the back, not finding anything else of importance.

Julie kept her car spotless, so I hadn't expected to find much.

I tucked my phone inside the backpack and threw it over my shoulder while easing the car door shut. "Let's go."

Just as I said the words a sound rumbled through the air, heading straight for us. Talon twisted around while moving to stand in front of me like he was going to protect me from the evils of the world. The gesture was touching, but like he said earlier, I was not an omega. Not anymore.

I pushed at his back. "We need to go. Now."

The pounding of paws against the ground made my heart race. We ran toward the back where we came in at. Anya and Talon went in different directions, and I guessed they were trying to get the dogs to follow them.

A deep growl echoed several feet behind me, and I pushed myself to run faster. I didn't want to have to kill a dog tonight, so I hoped I got out before they caught up with me.

The fence was about a yard ahead of me. Relief flooded me. I was going to make it. I heard the fence rattled and snapped my head to see both Anya and Talon climbing over it.

Just then a large massif stepped in my path, making me skid to a stop. My inner wolf snarled and flooded my system with her power. I held up my hands to the dog and slowly backed away. That was when I heard more growls behind me. Crap. I was trapped.

"Mattie," Talon yelled right before he jumped back over the fence and shifted into a large dog.

What the hey? I didn't sense that he was a shifter.

Two of the dogs to my right broke from the circle they formed around me and went after Talon. Fear pumped through me. "Stop!"

They all stopped and looked at me. All the dogs, Talon included. Even Anya stared at me.

Straightening, I studied each of the dogs. The massiff was the alpha of this group, so he was the one I needed to persuade to let me leave. "I am leaving and will not invade your territory again. You will let me go."

The massif cocked his head and stared at me for a long while before advancing toward me. I stood my ground and made eye contact with the massiff. When he reached me, he sniffed me, so I held out my hand. My wolf was close to the surface and the large male dog could sense her.

After a few more minutes, the massiff huffed then walked away. The other dogs followed him. All except Talon who shifted back to his human form, fully clothed. I found that disappointing.

"Are you okay?" He touched my face then my shoulders before running his hands down my arms.

I took his hands in mine and squeezed. "I'm fine. Why didn't you tell me you were a dog shifter?"

He laughed. "I'm not. I'll explain back at the apartment. We need to go before the owner of the place comes out shooting."

"We don't need that to happen." I went to the fence and climbed over. That time I paid attention so my hoodie wouldn't get stuck.

CHAPTER SEVEN

Despite the active night I had with my new friends and how late we stayed up while Anya cooked up the spell that would tell us what magic, if any, was used to kidnap Julie, I was wide awake as the sky brightened with the rising sun. It was too bad that I couldn't see the actual sunrise because we were on the west coast. But the sky went from dark to light with the blue filtering through the clouds. It was a beautiful sight.

So beautiful that I had to paint it.

I sat on a stool on my balcony with my easel and canvas, painting the city and the bay below. The smell of coffee drifted in the air, but I couldn't tell if it was coming from one of my neighbors or Talon's

Coffee House a block away. No matter where it came from it smelled divine.

Thoughts of Talon filled my mind and my wolf sighed. I didn't know what to do about him. Relationships weren't my area of expertise. In fact, I've never been intimate with anyone before. That was a little pathetic. I was forty-five and still a virgin.

A soft meow drew my attention from my painting and roaming thoughts to a small black cat walking across the top of the railing. "Well, hello, kitty."

I kept my voice soft so I wouldn't spook the kitty. I stood and went to the railing, then looked over. Hex Towers had thirty floors and I was on floor twenty-nine. How in the hey did the kitty get all the way up there? Fearing for the cat's life if she or he slipped off, I scooped it up and went inside. "I bet you are hungry."

Once inside my kitchen, which was open to the living room, I set the kitty on my counter then opened the fridge. I had milk, so I poured a little in a bowl and set it in front of her. Somehow, I sensed that she was a girl. After a quick peek, I smiled that I was right.

I stroked her head and ran my hand down her

back as she lapped up the milk. "I have some leftover chicken. Would you like some?"

She lifted her head from the bowl and meowed. That was a yes. Turning back to the fridge, I pulled out the chicken from last night's dinner and broken up a few pieces for Ms. Kitty and popped them in the microwave for a few seconds to knock the chill from it.

While Kitty ate her chicken, I dialed Anya's number. She answered on the first ring. "Sup."

"Hi. I need to go to the store."

"I'll be right over."

She hung up without saying bye, which was fine by me. She lived next door. A few seconds later a knock sounded on the door and I used my magic to unlock and open it. Anya walked in and froze halfway to the kitchen, then raised a brow at the cat on the counter eating her breakfast.

"Where did that cat come from?"

I pointed to the balcony door that was still open. "I was painting, and she just appeared. Isn't she pretty? I need a name for her."

Slowly Anya made her way to the island, eyeing Kitty the whole time. "You can't keep that cat."

"Why not?" I petted her again. The cat, not Anya. "Oh, do you think she belongs to someone?"

"Not at Hex Towers. I've never seen that cat before." Anya reached for her hand out tentatively like she wasn't sure if Kitty would bite her or not. Before petting her, Anya held her hand a few inches above her. The tension in Anya's posture melted away and she stroked the cat's back, making Kitty purr.

"Hey, she likes you."

"Of course, she does. What's not to like?" Anya laughed, then picked up my phone from the counter. "I'm going to put Simon's number in your contact list. He'll do your shopping for you. Felix doesn't want you out in public much until Julie is found."

I pursed my lips, not liking that Felix was starting to make demands and keep me locked up just like my uncle had. "Where is Felix?"

"He's in a meeting. It won't do any good arguing with him." Anya started playing with Kitty, getting her to chase her fingers across the counter.

"I know that, but that won't stop me from telling him how I feel about being locked away." I took Kitty's plate and bowl to the sink and rinsed them off before putting them in the dishwasher.

"He's not locking you up. You can leave, just not alone." Anya scooped Kitty up and carried her to the sofa.

Gathering my phone, I joined Anya on the couch. "So do I just call Simon and tell him what I need from the store?"

"You can or you can place your order with the store, and he can pick it up."

Nodding I decided to call Simon to introduce myself and see if he had a preference. He answered on the third ring. "Miss Matilda, is everything okay?"

His voice was deep and had a slight gravel sound to it. "Yes, everything is good. Anya gave me your number and said you will go shopping for me?"

There was a long pause. "She did?"

"You weren't aware of this?" I shot Anya a narrowed eyed look. She shrugged and started making kissy faces at Kitty. "I'll place an order and go get it later. It's not a big deal if you're busy."

"No. I'll go shopping. What do you need?"

"Are you sure?"

"Positive."

I told him about Kitty. "I'm not sure what they need. Food of course and a litter box. Oh, and toys. Nothing too small that she can choke on."

"A scratching post and maybe a cat tree," Anya added.

I wasn't sure I wanted a tree in my apartment,

but Simon said he heard Anya and got everything covered. "I'll see you an a few."

"Okay thanks!" I hung up and turned on the sofa and tucked one leg under me so I could face Anya. "Can I ask you something personal?"

"Sure."

I nibbled my bottom lip while considering what I wanted to know. "It's about Talon."

"Most definitely. What do you want to know?"

"Well, I'm not sure. I mean, everything." I studied my hands in my lap.

Anya covered those hands. "Just say what's on your mind."

"He's my mate," I whispered.

A wide smile spread across her face. "That's great."

"Yeah, I guess. I'm not sure I want him knowing right now. I just got out of a controlling situation. Plus, I've never dated anyone." I lifted both legs, bending them at the knees and hugging them to my chest.

Anya set Kitty down on the floor and placed a hand on my back. "Don't be ashamed of that. You weren't in a healthy pack."

"I'm not ashamed. Just nervous, I guess."

"Well, you have nothing to be nervous about.

Talon is your mate and I happen to know that he is so into you." Anya leaned into me so our shoulders touched.

"You think so?" I laid my head on her shoulder. Kitty crawled back on the couch and snuggled between us.

"I know so," Anya said as she scratched Kitty's head. "But you do need to sit him down and talk to him about this."

Yeah, eventually. "I will, but I need to find Julie first."

"Yes, Julie is our priority as are you. Speaking of, the spell should be ready now." She stood, taking my hand to pull me to a stand and drag me behind her as she entered the kitchen area.

She placed the ceramic bowl with the potion in it in the corner and had it covered with a cheesecloth. I hadn't dared look at it. I was afraid that I'd contaminate it.

Anya grabbed the bowl and carried it to the island, then uncovered it. Instantly, I clamped a hand over my mouth and nose. An awful smell drift up from the bowl that reminded me of a skunk and rotting flesh. "That's awful."

"I know. It's worse than I thought." She pointed to the bowl, and I peeked inside.

"It turned brown. What does that mean?"

Anya went to the sink, put the stopper in the drain, then turned the water on. Then she added two handfuls of salt into the water. "It means dark magic was used. Do you have a small amber jar?"

I shook my head, but I conjured one and handed it to her. "Dark magic?" Fear flooded my insides.

"It's not Julie's magic. I'm not sure what it is." She held the jar above the brown sneaky goop and used her magic to move droplets of the stuff into the jar. "I'll take this sample to my mom. She'll know."

"Could I go with you?"

"Sure." Anya stuffed the small jar into her pocket, then dumped the bowl of brown goop into the sink full of saltwater. Within seconds the horrid smell vanished, and the water turned milky. Salt neutralizes magic.

"Cool. I'm going to go change and bring in the easel." I made it halfway to my bedroom when I remembered Kitty. "What about the cat?"

Anya glanced at the feline, who was playing with a twist tie that I had no idea where she found it. "Bring her with us. Mom will help name her."

Glee filled me and I might have squealed a little as I went out onto the balcony. I cleaned up my paints and then carried them and the easel into my room to, then dressed in a pair of comfy jeans and a lavender cashmere sweater.

By the time I emerged from my room, Simon was there with the loot from the pet store. He went all out too.

Simon was a large guy—tall with wide shoulder and arms that were bigger than one of my thighs. His skin was a dark brown and he shaved his head. He smiled at me, revealing the tips of his fangs and held out his hand. "It is a pleasure to meet you."

"Like wise, "I said and shook his hand, then motioned to the bags on the floor. "That's a lot for one little kitty."

That kitty in question was rumbling inside one of the bags. She found a small mouse made of a soft fabric and started batting it around the living room. I watched her play for a little bit until Anya came to stand beside me.

"Mom will stop by here. She was on her way to my place anyway."

"Cool." I sat on the floor and started going through the bags. There was a big box near the door. "What's that?"

"Cat tree," Simon said as he pulled out a pock-etknife to open the box.

Ah, so a cat tree wasn't an actual tree. It was a

good thing I didn't say that out loud earlier. It was times like this I hated my uncle more than usual for keeping me confined to pack land. I never got to explore the world or learn things that people my age should know.

I truly lived a sheltered life. Not anymore.

I was free to explore. Free to learn. Free to have friends and to love. The latter was something I wanted. That was if Talon would want me.

CHAPTER EIGHT

I didn't know what to expect when meeting Anya's mom, Sage. I knew she'd be a witch because Anya was. I wasn't prepared for the amount of power coming off her. Nor was I prepared for her to repeat the word the old witch did moments before she shoved me into that closet portal.

Sorceress.

Sage had to be confused. I wasn't a sorceress. My mom was a wolf and as far as I know my dad was a witch. Then again who knew. He died before I was born.

Holding the small amber jar with the dark magic goop up at the light, Sage drew her brows and scrunched her nose. "This is old magic. Far beyond my existence."

Then she pulled the cork from the jar, and I held my breath. But watching Sage wave the jar under her nose brought back memories of what it smelled like. My wolf whimpered and put her paws over her head.

Trust me, it's far worse on my end.

It gets worse? I snorted at her comment and remembered I wasn't alone. Some people thought it was weird that I talked to my wolf when I couldn't shift. They said it was unnatural. Some pack mates said I was crazy. I let them believe that because it was sometimes safer for people to fear you.

So, I played the crazy card most my life.

"Oh, this is bad," Sage made a soured face as she placed the cork back in place.

I nodded, agreeing. The magic used was bad. My own magic even backed away at the scent. "What does it mean?"

Was Julie dead? No. I refuse to believe that. She was alive and I was going to find her.

"I don't know," Sage said and then met her daughter's gaze. "Is this all of it?"

Anya nodded once. "I poured the rest in salt water. It turned milky."

"Good. I'll consult with the coven to see if anyone can identify the magical signature. Or at least an origin to start tracing. Whoever is using this type of magic is not our friend. I'm sure Felix is aware." Sage slipped the jar into her coat pocket then twirled her fingers over the pocket. I recognized the magic as a protection spell.

Anya moved to the door to walk her mom out. "Yes, he is aware. It is Julie who is missing. We got that signature from her car."

Sage sighed and took both of Anya's hands. "Tell him if he needs anything, the coven is here for him."

"I will, Mom. Thanks."

Sage kissed Anya on the cheek and opened the door. "I'll see myself out. It was nice meeting you Mattie."

She was gone before I opened my mouth. Just as Anya pushed the door close it opened again and Talon entered.

And he brought food. Chinese.

Anya and I took the food bags from him and started spreading everything out on the kitchen island. Talon grabbed the plates.

Just then Simon walked out of my room with the black kitty on his heals. Crap I forgot he was still here. "Hey, you hungry? Talon brought enough for a pack of wolves."

Talon turned around to face me. "No, just one wolf."

I grinned. "I don't eat that much."

I totally did and was thankful for a fast metabolism.

Talon chuckled and booped my nose. "Sure, you don't."

"Are they always like this?" Simon asked.

Anya, said, "Yeah."

"I think it's great that she found her mate."

I jerked my gaze to Simon's in horror. "What?" That's it, play dumb.

Talon stared at me, and I closed my eyes. Okay, I was not going to freak out. One side, the cat was out of the bag, and I didn't have to tell him. On the other hand, he could reject me on the spot.

"Why is Simon here anyway?" Talon asked.

"He was setting up the stuff in the bedroom for Kitty." I moved to walk into the living room, but the Kitty stepped into my path. I scooped her up and showed her to Talon. "Meet Kitty."

Talon's gaze lingered on my face for a few before looking at the black cat in my arms. "She's a cutie." He reached out and scratched under her chin and she purred.

Talon opened his mouth like he wanted to say something but his phone chimed, distracting him. He pulled it from his pocket and stared at it for a few. His brows bunched as he worked his jaw. He might have been grinding his teeth. I couldn't really tell, but I had the sinking feeling whatever text he got wasn't good.

Meeting my gaze, he said, "That was River, my brother. He said there was a body found about a mile from where they found Julie's car."

I gasped and covered my mouth. My lungs burned as I exhaled while tears blurred my vision. It couldn't be Julie. I tried to speak, to ask if they identified the body, but words wouldn't form.

Kitty reached up and patted my face. I glanced down at her and held her close. Talon moved closer and rubbed my arm. Instantly, I leaned into him. He kept his voice low. "I hate to ask, but River wants you to come down to the morgue and ID the body."

I nodded, still not able to form words. The body couldn't be Julie. As much as I didn't want to, I had to go and make sure it wasn't her. Turning, I went into the bedroom to show Kitty where all her things were.

As soon as I set her down on the floor, she went

straight to her food bowl, ate a few bites, then darted off to check out her litter box.

"Wow, it's like cat haven in here," Talon said, standing at the door.

"Yeah, Simon went a little overboard." I looked up and Simon was standing behind Talon.

"I'll be going with you guys, but I'll hang back," Simon said as he moved to the door.

Anya waved. "I'll ride with Simon."

"Okay, bye." I met Talon's gaze and grinned. Or at least I hoped I did. My emotions were all over the place. It wouldn't be too far-fetched that my face betrayed them all.

Talon took Kitty from me and sat her in her bed. He was so gentle with her it made my heart melt. When he straightened, he smirked at me. "What?"

"Nothing." I averted my gaze and exited the bedroom, which meant I had to push past him to get out. He definitely didn't make it easy for me to escape. "I'm ready to get this over with."

THE DRIVE to the morgue was quiet. I was glad that Talon didn't quiz me about being my mate. Maybe he was waiting for me to bring it up, which I plan to, just not until we find Julie. Yes, find her because I refuse to believe she was dead.

But walking into the building had my stomach in knots. My wolf paced inside me with worry.

Talon moved closer and placed a hand on my lower back. His touch sent a wave of desire through me, but it also helped to ease my anxiety. Support and sympathy flowed into me through his touch as we entered the room where the body was.

The body laid on a gurney with a white sheet over her. My heart slowed to almost a stop and I felt like I was going to be sick.

Taking a deep breath, I calmed myself and advanced to the body. Just then a man in black dress slacks and a white button down entered the room. His blond hair covered the tops of his ears, but it was his blue eyes and facial features that told me he was Talon's brother.

I could tell that River was younger than Talon, but I wasn't sure how many years separated them. If I had to guess, it'd be no more than ten years. It was hard to tell with supernatural beings though. There was the whole aging slower than humans thing.

Holding out his hand, River said, "You must be Mattie. Talon has told me very little about you."

I shook his hand. "In his defense, we just met."

River gestured to the body, his features taking a sad, darker tone. "Are you ready?"

"Yeah." I had the urge to just ripped the sheet away like a bandage. If you're quick about the ripping off, it hurt less.

Although in this case it would hurt no matter what if Julie was under that sheet.

River apparently was thinking the same thing because he pulled back the sheet quickly. When my eyes fell on the face of the woman, I sagged in relief. Then I felt bad about being relieved. It wasn't Julie, but the unknown woman had bruising around her neck and one side of her face. Her death was not painless.

"That's not Julie." I grabbed Talon's hand and held it.

Anya entered the room. "Thank the gods." Then she frowned as she moved closer to the body. "Do you smell that?"

My immediate reaction was to say no, but then sniffed the air. The faint notes of rotting flesh. I dismissed it when I entered the room because it was a morgue. I've never been to one before, so I figured that scent was normal.

I leaned closer and lifted the sheet. That was

when the horrid smell filled my senses, making my eyes water. "It's dark magic."

"Just like what was found in the car." Anya hugged her waist and turned to River. "Whoever killed this woman, also has Julie."

CHAPTER NINE

Talon had to work a shift at his coffee shop because one of his baristas had a sick child. I could tell he didn't want to leave me, but I assured him that I was fine. After serval moment of hesitation he left.

I wasn't alone. Anya was there and my new kitty.

"Have you thought of a name for her?" Anya wiggled a string in the air for Kitty to play with it.

"No. Do you have any suggestions? I've never had a pet before, especially not a cat." My old pack would have killed a cat, so I hadn't dared to get one.

"What about Trixie?"

"I like that." I scooped Trixie up and rubbed noses with her. "Do you like the name Trixie?"

She let out a soft meow, then purred. That was a yes. "Trixie it is, then!"

After another few moments, Trixie wiggled in my arms, wanting down to chase the string some more. I let her go play and studied Anya for a few. "What can we do to find Julie?"

"Unfortunately, not a whole lot. Felix has people out looking for her and has spread the word through the paranormal communities to report to him with anything suspicious. This recent murder is new..." She jerked her head up and added, "We can see who that woman was and start researching her disappearance."

"I'm in. Where do we start?" If we actively worked on the case, I would feel like I was doing something to find my best friend. Julie had been my only friend until I moved to Seattle.

Wow. It's only been a few days, but it seems so much longer. I not only had new friends, but protectors, and found my mate.

Anya pulled out her phone and pushed a number in and placed it on speaker.

"Chief Marcs."

Until right then I didn't know Talon's last name. Marcs. Talon Marcs. I giggled at the sound of it. At the same time, I wanted to hug him because he was most likely teased as a kid with that name.

Assuming that Talon and River had the same last name.

"Hey, River. Have you ID'd the Jane Doe yet?" Anya glanced at me with a raised brow. She must likely want to know where my thoughts went. I shook my head.

There was a long pause before River answered Anya's question. "Not yet, but she's a demon. I tried a spell to identify her, but it didn't take."

Anya frowned. "Yeah, I should have told you earlier, but don't mix your magic with the power coating the body. It's old bad magic. I have Mom looking into the signature, but I'm not hopeful that will help us. Can you keep the body protected from the humans for a while? Mattie and I are going to hunt down her family and see if there are any other missing paras in recent months."

"I thought Felix was working on that." River's tone turned a little more serious from when he first picked up the phone.

Anya crossed her eyes, making me laugh. "He is and we're helping. If you hear anything shoot me a text."

She hung up before River had a chance to

comment further about us getting involved. "At least we have a species to start with."

Excitement bubbled up. A mystery to solve with possible danger. That was right up my ally. I held out my hands and conjured a small laptop with a charger. I couldn't forget that. I jumped up and rushed to the desk in my room to set up the computer and plug it in.

Anya followed me in and sat on the end of my bed. My wolf tugged at me to look at her, but I ignored the animal. I didn't care that Anya sat on my bed, but my wolf had become obsessed with keeping other scents off our linen and blankets. She hated every wolf in the pack. Well, I did too but not to the extreme she did. It was a good thing my uncle seemed to agree with me on keeping everyone out of my room and my space.

Pushing away those thoughts, I finally turned and frowned. She sat on the very edge of the bed, almost standing, awkwardly. "You can sit on the mattress."

She watched me for a few and slowly sat a little further on the bed. "Do you sense my wolf?"

Anya shrugged and relaxed. "When I came into the room, she sent out a low pulse of energy. A warning."

And it was. I tried to keep her from doing it but old habits and all that. "Old habit. She doesn't mean anything by it. We're working on it."

There was a long silence, so I moved us right along to the reason we are in my bedroom. "If you give me some basic information on demons, I can run some searches."

One corner of Anya's mouth lifted. "What kind of searches will you be running Agent?"

I snorted. "How do you think I survived forty-five years in a pack of rogue wolves? Blackmail keeps them in line. If it didn't, then I showed them who the alpha really was. I didn't have to do that often. In fact, I believe it only happened once. That was disappointing."

Laughing, Anya said, "Yeah, I can see how both methods would have worked. How could they treat you like an omega? I knew you were powerful the moment we met. You are both an alpha and sorceress. That mix is very powerful. Some would say it's dangerous."

There was a warning in her tone, and I agreed with that warning. "Julie and I knew the risks when we made the decision to do it. My time there was running out. My magic is getting stronger, and my wolf wanted to kill everyone in the pack, starting with my uncle. I really didn't want to be the first Alpha to slaughter her own pack."

And I said all that out loud. Anya was for sure to think I was insane. Instead of looking at me like the devil herself, she said, "I'm sure Julie would have helped with the slaughtering."

"You got that right."Trixie jumped up on the bed and rubbed her head against Anya's arm. Anya scratched her head as she told me about demons. "The demons that live in Seattle are under Felix's rule, like most factions in the area, so digging into the families won't be that hard."

Then she rattled off a website that ended up being a database of the factions and their families. "Felix likes to keep tabs on who comes and goes, but he doesn't check in with each family. Basically, if they aren't drawing attention to themselves or breaking the rules, he lets them be."

In other words Felix would never know if one of them were kidnapped or murdered unless the family lets him know. "Is there a demon leader that we could possibly talk to?"

"Xel'gall. We call him Xel for short." Anya started texting. After a few minutes, she said, "He'll see us in a couple of hours."

That was easy. "Just like that?"

"Yep. The factions all respect Felix, so when he or his enforcers ask for something they usually agree without question. Although Xel will not make the interview easy. He likes to play games." Anya rolled her eyes.

Turning in my seat, I picked up my sketch book and pencil, then started drawing the female demon from the morgue.

Anya left to go pick up a few things from her apartment and to check in with Felix. I was too focused on my sketch to acknowledge that she left. I think I did wave, though.

I finished the drawing and studied it for a few. There was something missing, and I couldn't pinpoint what it was.

Someone knocked on my door, so I stretched out my senses to see who it was. Anya and Talon. I smiled and called out. "It's open." Standing, I went into my huge walk-in closet. My room at my uncle's pack was small and didn't have a closet. All my things were stuffed into a chest. Having all this space to myself was amazing. Of course, I didn't have much stuff to fill the large closet, but that gave me something to look forward to. The little bit of clothes in there were gifts from Felix.

I dressed in a pair of black jeans and a long

sleeve t-shirt with Talon's Coffee House logo on the front. Once I slipped my shoes on, I grabbed my sketchbook and exited my room. "Hi," I said to Talon and handed him the sketch. "Something doesn't seem right about it."

"Wow. That looks exactly like her." Talon looked over the drawing before handing it back to me. "Her eyes seem a little off, but it's hard to tell since they were closed when we saw her."

I glanced back at him and nodded. "You're right. But is it good enough that Xel will recognize her?"

"Xel?" Talon looked from me to Anya.

"Oh, Anya didn't tell you? We have a meeting with the demon king to ask about this female. We're hoping it will lead us to clues about where Julie could be or at least who has her." I moved to the coat rack near the door where I kept my messenger bag.

After slipping my sketchbook inside the bag, I turned to Anya and Talon. "I'm ready."

CHAPTER TEN

Xel didn't live in the city, he lived in the mountains. And on a farm. At least it looked that way. Chickens and a few roosters roamed around the yard. I got out of Talon's SUV and was assailed by several different sounds. I heard horses and cows in the distance and some pigs.

The house was a beautiful two-story farmhouse with a wraparound porch. It had a metal roof. It was all so human-like that I found it unbelievable that the king of the demons lived there.

The sound of the front door opening, drew my attention to a man wearing a cowboy hat. Of course, he had other clothing on. He wore a light green button-down and a pair of blue jeans. On his feet were, yep, you guessed it, cowboy boots.

Anya stopped next to me and laughed softly. "Xel transferred from Texas to Seattle about a year ago. He brought his home state with him."

The demon in the Stetson stepped forward to lean against the railing. He was a large guy and all muscle. He was also not bad looking. Some would say he was hot, but he really didn't do anything for me. That had nothing to do with him being a demon and everything to do with me finding my mate.

Speaking of...Talon moved closer to me and placed his hand on my back. At first, I froze, waiting for my wolf's reaction. Generally, she didn't like males touching us, but the crazy beast curled up right against Talon's hand.

By the way he caressed the spot with his finger told me he sensed my wolf. That was interesting. I filed that away for later.

"Are y'all going to stand there staring all day?" Xel had a southern draw to his voice, and I couldn't figure out if it was fake or not.

Anya was the first one of us to advance up the steps to the porch. Talon insisted I go next. I made sure I put a little more wiggle in my step, teasing my mate.

Xel walked inside in front of Anya and led us through the living room to a room in back corner. His office. It was pretty big. I guess it had to be if he did his demon king duties from there.

He sat behind his desk and gestured for us to sit as well. "What can I help you with?"

That was my cue to pull out my sketch and hand it over. "She was found dead yesterday."

Anya filled him in on everything - Julie, the stinky old magic, and our theories, which wasn't much.

It was a long few seconds before Xel spoke. "That is Stacy. She is...was a good demon. She helped anyone, no matter the species. I didn't even know she was missing."

"Sorry," I muttered softly. He liked the female but not in a romantic way.

"It's not your fault, little witch." Xel waved his hand and a thick old-looking leather-bound book materialized. Using his powers, he opened it and the pages flipped rapidly, suddenly stopping. Xel narrowed his eyes, then looked up at me while handing the book off to Anya.

"I've known of one power that carries the signature that you described. There was one particular family bloodline that had kind of dark magic." Xel watched me the whole time he spoke, sending an uneasiness through me.

Anya made a sound that I couldn't decipher, then said, "The Valgards."

It was obvious that Anya knew of this family line by the fear that washed away all the color from her face. "Who are the Valgards?"

"The most powerful family of sorcerers. Legends say they were the first of their kind," Talon answered.

Anya nodded slowly and closed the book before handing it back to Xel. "They were all killed."

Xel fixed his gaze on me. "Not all of them, apparently."

An uneasy feeling surfaced while my wolf snarled at him. She didn't like the sudden attention he was giving us. There was accusation in his depths, and I didn't understand why.

What I did understand was that whoever took Julie and killed Stacy, was part of this all-powerful ancient sorcerer family. "Why would a sorcerer kill a demon and kidnap a fae?"

I hadn't expected anyone to know the answer, which was good because none of us did. The question was more of a pondering thing than an actual inquire. To get the wheels going.

Before anyone said anything, Anya's, Talon's, and my phone chimed at the same time. We checked our phones. I knew they got the same message from Felix.

Urgent meeting at my place.

My heart started beating faster than it ever had. Dread sank like a rock in my soul.

Anya stood and did a little bow to Xel. Out of respect, so did I while Anya said, "That's the boss. We have to go but if you remember anything or find out something, let us know."

Xel rose to his feet and followed us to the door. "Like wise. If you find out who did this before I do, make him hurt."

"This SOB took Felix's mate, he will hurt." Anya softened her tone and took Xel's hand. "I'm sorry about Stacy. Was she family?"

"Not biological. Everyone on this ranch is family." Xel opened the door for us. "Don't keep Felix waiting for too long."

Definitely didn't want to do that.

WHEN WE GOT BACK to Hex Towers, we rode the elevator to the top floor. The penthouse. Felix's living quarters was the entire top floor.

I've only seen the inside of Felix office once via a

video chat he and Julie were doing when I first met her. There was a lot of black and dark-colored wood. Standing in his living room, I took in all the random artwork and relics he must have collected over the years. It was random. Nothing matched, except that every piece was an oddity.

Talon leaned down until his lips brushed my ear, sending a warm shiver through my body. "Felix collects weird things."

"I like to collect things that remind me of the places I've been." Felix entered the room and motioned for us all to sit. "I received this note a few moments before I messaged the three of you."

He handed the note to me, and I read it with disbelief. It was a ransom note demanding a million dollars for the safe return of Julie. "You got to be kidding me. A million bucks? That's an insult to Julie."

And too much money to just hand over to a crazy sorcerer.

"I will be meeting him and making the exchange," Felix announced.

I handed the note to Anya. "I'm going too."

"Not happening"

"No way."

Both of those statements were said at the same

time by Talon and Felix. Talon spoke the latter. I rolled my eyes and crossed my arms as I sat back on the sofa. "Julie wouldn't be in this mess if I didn't want to escape my uncle. This is my fault."

"It's not your fault. The idea to fake your death was mine. Julie formed the plan and brought you into it. It's no one's fault." Felix stared at me for a long while and I stared back.

He broke the eye contact first. "Fine. Simon!"

The enforcer entered the living room from the hallway to our right. He smiled at me and asked, "How is Ms. Kitty?"

"She is good and has a name. Trixie."

Felix frowned. "You have a cat?" When I nodded, he said, "But you're a wolf?"

"My wolf loves cats. She hates other wolves." I didn't need to explain that because Felix knew all about my life. Shaking his head, he brought us back to the subject matter. "Simon, I need you to put together a small team who will be with Mattie and Talon. I'll call this asshat and arrange the ransom drop. Simon and Anya will be at my side during the drop because I'm not stupid enough to go without my guards. Mattie and Talon and the team will be behind a cloaking spell and hang back in case everything goes to hell."

We all nodded in agreement. It was a solid plan I guessed. Not that there was much more we could do.

It's a trap.

Yep, I agreed with my wolf. This sounded too easy. The kidnapper killed a demon, but wants to let Julie go for one million dollars? None of this added up to me. "You know this is a trap, right?"

Felix locked gazes with me and smiled wickedly. "I'm counting on it."

CHAPTER ELEVEN

Since leaving Felix's penthouse I'd been antsy. Waiting had never been an issue for me, but this was Julie's life we were trying to save.

Anya stayed behind, leaving Talon and me alone for the first time since Simon spilled my secret that Talon was my mate. Well, it might not have been a secret. It was possible that Talon sensed I was his mate just as I did.

"Did you want something to eat or drink?" I started to the kitchen, but Talon beat me to it.

"Go sit, I'll make us a snack. It's still too early for dinner." When I didn't move, he turned me around and gently pushed me toward the sofa.

The heat of his hands seeped into my skin, and I loved it. So did my wolf. I went to my room and kicked off my shoes. Movement on the bed caught my attention. Trixie sat on top of a duffle bag that wasn't there when I left earlier. She meowed and pawed at the bag.

Drifting over, I petted her head and scratched under her chin and inspected the bag. A few scents were on it: Mine, Julie's, and Simon's. Then I remembered Julie was supposed to grab the bag from my room at my uncle's while everyone was distracted with my sudden death.

It must had been in the trunk of her car. I didn't think to look when we went to the impound yard.

I opened the bag and was hit with the smell of dark magic. "That is a horrid smell."

Trixie meowed and placed her paw over her nose. I was right there with her. There was only one thing to do. Everything in inside the bag and the bag itself was getting a salt bath.

I entered the kitchen and grabbed a box of salt and went to the bathroom where I filled the tub with cold water, then dumped the salt in. While the tub was filling, I grabbed the bag of clothes from my room.

When I reentered the bathroom, Talon was in there. "What are you doing?"

I held up the bag, then dumped all the contents

into the tub of water. "Simon brought this up while we were visiting the demon cowboy. I'm guessing it was in Julie's car because it smells like that bad magic." And the scent turned my stomach. It was all I could do to stop from making gagging sounds.

I did shudder.

As if smelling it for the first time, Talon cupped his hand over his nose. "I'm going to open the balcony door."

"Good thinking." I turned off the water and conjured a large wooden spoon to stir the clothes, bag, and salt water together. It was a good thing I didn't pack any of my other personal belongings. Julie said it was best to only bring a few clothes and leave everything else. It would be more believable that way.

She had a point, plus I didn't want any reminders of my past life. I was starting over.

Exiting the bathroom, I stopped halfway to the sofa. Talon had just set a large plate with cheeses and meats on the coffee table. He looked up at me and curled his finger in a come here gesture. My heart kicked up a few beats per second. My intuition told me we were about to have *the talk*. The mating talk.

I sat beside him and grabbed a few pieces of cheese, waiting for him to ask his questions.

"At first I was shocked, but the more I think about it, I realize that I knew I was your mate all along." He picked up my hand and held it. The one without the cheese in it.

"I knew when I first saw you at your coffee house."

"Why didn't you say anything?"

I shrugged and nibbled on the corner of a cheese square, thinking of how to explain it without seeming like I didn't want a mate. Because I did. Just not when my life was so upside down. "I want to take it slow. I'm not ready for a mate, yet here you are. Things are so weird right now and for the first time in my life I have a chance to discover who I am and who I want to be."

We locked gazes and held each other's stare for a while. Then he lifted my hand to his lips to press a kiss to the tips of my fingers. "I understand. From what you told me about your uncle and now we're focused on finding Julie..."

"Yeah, it's a lot."

He sat back, taking me with him so I cuddled into his side. It felt amazing to be wrapped in his arms. "This is nice."

"Have you ever had a boyfriend?"

My cheeks heated and I didn't want to answer

him. Was I too old to be that inexperienced? But I couldn't lie to him, so I hid my face in his shirt as I answered. "No. I lived a sheltered life. Roger had me followed wherever I went. I didn't even bother with entertaining the idea of having a boyfriend. I was sure Roger would kill him on the spot."

Talon drew random designs on my hip as he spoke. "Fear makes us do things to keep everyone around us safe. We forget to include self-care along the way."

He was so right. "So, you aren't scared off at the fact that you are my mate? That's pretty permanent. Lifetime commitment."

He flashed a sexy smile. "I like that you want to take it slow. Plus, we have plenty of time to get to know each other."

We sure did.

CHAPTER TWELVE

I t was just after dinner when Felix sent a group message to me, Talon, and his enforcers about the drop time. Anxiety was raging like a wildfire inside me. I couldn't stop fidgeting on the drive to the spot Felix was meeting the kidnapper.

We had a name now. Otis Richards. When Talon and I dug into the man's background, we were confused that there was nothing that proved he was anything but human. His name didn't come up on any of the factions' databases. So how did a human come across ancient magic that smelled like Satan's dirty gym socks.

It didn't make sense. "Otis has to be paranormal. Julie could overpower a human."

"He could have made a deal with a demon.

Rogues exist in all species," said as he followed Felix's car.

Anya and Simon were riding with Felix, as his guards for the drop. Felix had told Otis that was nonnegotiable. Then gave the human or whatever he was the other choice was a full swarm of vampires invading his home.

Felix ruled like a mafia boss. I even thought that the organized crime factions answer to Felix, human or not.

And that was why I was safe. Even if Roger found out I faked my death and came looking for me, my uncle would not leave the city of Seattle alive.

I was more than okay with that.

"How much further?" My wolf was pacing and muttering. There were times like these where she felt caged in. It broke my heart because I wanted her to be free. It wasn't from the lack of trying.

"The next turn." Talon reached over and covered my hand. "We'll get her back."

A sigh slipped from my lips as my wolf slowed her pacing. Talon's touch calmed her and me. "I know. My wolf doesn't have the best patience."

He winked at me, then released my hand to make the turn down a narrow residential road. We drove a ways down the dark street and turned again at a dead end. After a few blocks, he cut his lights and slowed, letting Felix's car go into the next section of the neighborhood first while I did a cloaking spell to hide not only the vehicle and us, but the sound of the engine as well. To Otis or anyone else who happened to notice would only see that Felix's car was the only one there.

Talon parked on the side of the street across from the meeting place. "A children's playground?"

Talon chuckled. "Yeah. I'm betting Otis lives in this neighborhood or the next one over."

"Not very bright, is he?"

"I'm going with no."

We laughed, then jumped as the back doors opened and two large vampires got in. I jerked around in my seat and growled. They froze, looking at me wide eye before glancing at Talon. "Who are you and how can you see us?"

That was when I heard Anya curse outside the SUV. She stuck her head in the vehicle. "Sorry. I led them here. Felix wants two guards in here with you."

She waited a beat before introducing the two vampires. "This is Cary and Finn."

I stared at them, and they stared back. I glared, they glared. Then I crossed my eyes, and everyone started laughing. They passed my wolf's test. We'll stare at those who are being jerks to us or startle us like these creeps. Most beings can't hold an alpha's stare for long. My experience the only ones that could hold my stare without a flicker of wanting to submit turned out to be great allies. So far, only Julie, Anya, Talon, Felix, and now Cary and Finn can do it.

"We cool?" Anya said with a grin and a thumbs up.

"Yeah, we're good." I waved her off and straighten in my seat.

I watched Anya dart across the street to walk beside Felix. Otis was nowhere in sight. I scanned the houses and the area around us, noting every shadow.

After a few minutes a black car pulled up behind Felix's car. It sat there for a while with the lights on. "What is he doing?"

My window was down so we could hear what was going on. Well, the vamps and I could, I wasn't sure how much Talon could hear. Witches had better hearing and other senses than humans, but not as good as shifters and vampires.

All I heard was the rumbling of Otis's car engine. I gripped my door handle ready to jump out just as the lights on the car shut off. Then a short stalky man got out of the car with two larger men. "Are those demons with him?"

Talon and the two vamps in the backseat said, "Yep."

They even popped the P at the end of the word. It made me giggle.

I took my phone out and snapped a few pictures. "Xel will be happy to have something to feed his pigs."

"That was a visual I didn't need," Talon said while chuckling.

I slipped the phone back into my pocket and scented the air. "Julie is not here." I pressed the ear piece Felix insisted we wear and repeated it. "Julie is not here. He has demons on his payroll."

"I am aware," Felix replied. His voice was calm, but it had an edge to it.

When Otis and his guards stopped, Felix asked where Julie was. Otis didn't move. "She's tied up at the moment and couldn't make it."

"A deal was a deal," Felix growled.

I sure hoped Felix didn't believe the chubby little weasel would actually hold up his side of the bargain. My question was why did Otis show up in the first place? Especially if he didn't intend on handing Julie over. Did he know who he was dealing with?

"This dude has a death wish."

I glanced at the vampires in the backseat to see which one spoke. It was Cary. I've seen him once before. It was when Felix visited Julie in Abbotsford last winter. At the time, Cary's shoulder length wavy brown hair was shorter. "I agree and I'm about to grant that wish if he doesn't start talking."

Just then Felix's voice came through our ear pieces. "I'm done here. You obviously know nothing about Julie or her whereabouts."

That statement snapped my focus back on them. Felix was bluffing. It's what he did when he wasn't getting what he wanted. That and use the dirt he dug up as blackmail. Hey, who do you think taught me to blackmail others?

And I'll do what I need to, to survive.

Otis laughed, making me growl at the little round man. "You are outnumbered in power."

Oh no he wasn't. I opened the SUV door and ignored Talon as he reached for me and the two vamps in the backseat as they called for me to get back in the SUV. My defiance made the three of them exit the vehicle and follow me across the street.

It wasn't until we stood behind Felix that I lowered our cloaking spell.

Otis's eyes grew huge, and he stared at me with his mouth open for a few seconds. Then he pointed at me. "You."

Yep, it was me. Now that I was face to face with him, I realized a few things. One, he was not fully human. He had magic coursing through him. My first guess was a witch, but it felt vaguely familiar to me. I couldn't figure out why.

Two, he wasn't all that sane. I felt a deep sadness rolling off him. That was something I knew all too well. I felt the same sadness when my mom died. Otis was still grieving his loved ones.

That didn't mean I felt sorry for him. I lost both my parents. One of those I never knew so I didn't really care about him. But my mom's death ripped a hole in my soul.

The third thing I noticed was he seemed to know me. Or at least thought he did. I've never seen him before in my life.

I looked over at the demons and smiled. "Hi, guys. I had the best meeting with Xel this morning. He will be so thrilled that you are out making friends. I texted him pics."

They glanced at each other, then vanished. That

was something I wasn't expecting. Demons could teleport. Who knew? Not me.

I placed my attention on Otis. "Where is Julie?"

"She is somewhere you will never sense. Too many scents to detect hers. And no magic can penetrate the area." Otis stood a little taller like he put me in my place. Little did he know about me.

I stepped forward and raised my hand. "Then I can just pull the information out of your mind."

Fear flooded his dark depths, and then he ran to his car like his ass was on fire.

I went to run after him, when Talon wrapped an arm around my waist and picked me up off the ground. "I know where she is," he whispered in my ear as he carried me back to the SUV.

He put me in the passenger seat and buckled me up. "We're going to go get her."

"Hell yes. Hang on Julie, we are coming for you."

CHAPTER THIRTEEN

"How do you know where she is?" I grabbed the door handle as Talon took the corners like a Rally race car driver. I felt like I need to yell out directions, only I had no clue where we were going.

"When he said she was somewhere no magic could detect, I knew. Felix definitely would know, so I'm counting on him following us."

So was I. However, I wasn't sure I wanted to face the vampire king right now. There was no doubt in my mind that his undies were in a bunch because Talon and I ran off to check out the location without guards.

Well, Felix would get over it.

Eventually.

"Are you going to tell me where she is? I suck at this guessing game because I'm not from here." I grinned, then cursed softly when he took another sharp turn.

"She's at The Loophole. It's a nightclub owned by one of the oldest fae families to live in Seattle. The club is open to all and is charmed so no magic can be used while inside." Talon slowed, then turned into a parking lot. A large neon sign with The Loophole lit up the lot.

The building reminded me of an old Scottish castle. The stone exterior was dark grey. There were no windows on the first two floors and the few that were on the upper levels were frosted with a purple light shining from within. It was creepy and beautiful at the same time.

I got out of the SUV and scanned the area. Even though there were a lot of scents around, Otis didn't know that I learned from a young age how to dive deep into my senses and detect the slight smells. If anyone could find Julie, it was me.

Moving toward the building, I took a deep breath, taking in all the scents. My wolf sorted through them all, searching for Julie's. Even a small note would put me on her trail.

My mom used to tell me I was a born tracker. Hunting was something I'd always been good at.

Julie had an earthy scent mixed with wild berries and mint. It was an odd combination, but it worked on her.

Catching some earthy notes, I picked up my pace to the side of the building. Talon had to jog to catch up with me. "Where are you going?"

"Tracking scents." I stopped when I heard Felix's car pull into the parking lot. "Oh, goody, Felix is here."

Talon glanced at the car as it pulled to a stop next to his SUV. "This should be fun."

Anya was the first one out of the car and she ran over to us. "You are in so much trouble."

I grinned and said loud enough Felix could hear. "Julie is here."

Felix's frown deepened. "So is Otis."

I glanced at the black car near the front door of the club. I saw it there and figured he'd be here. "Yeah, well he is no match for the four of us plus several enforcers."

Felix stepped into my space, and I straightened my spine and lifted my chin because he was a giant to me, and I had to look up to meet his gaze. "Go back to the SUV with Simon."

Not a fat chance in Hell. I rooted my feet in place and stared up at the alpha male vampire. "I'm not leaving."

"I'm trying to keep you safe."

"I'm a big girl, I can take care of myself. I've been doing it since Mom died." My wolf added a growl to the end of my statement. Too bad the only person to hear it was me. "Besides, I'm the only one that can sniff her out."

Felix stared into my eyes for a long moment before turning his attention to Talon. "Stay at her side."

"I plan to." Talon rubbed my back.

"Now that we settled that, do any of you know if there is a basement or a hidden room or somewhere around here that Otis could hide her?"

Just then the side door to The Loophole opened and Tania stuck her head out. The beautiful fae I met on my first day in Seattle studied each of us for a second. Her raven black hair was pulled back in a high ponytail with strands loose to frame her face. "What are you doing?"

"My friend Julie is missing, and we think she is here somewhere." I glanced at Anya, noting how she was avoiding eye contact with Tania.

Tania stepped outside and closed the door. "Why would you think she was here?"

Felix filled her in on Otis and Julie being missing and what lead us here. Tania frowned. "No one can break the enchantment on this place. That makes me wonder if he used it to hide her. But that still doesn't answer how he did it without my family knowing."

"Your family?" I asked.

Talon answered first, "Tania's family owns The Loophole."

Oh, that was cool.

"However, there is one place he could have accessed." Tania waved us to follow her behind the club and to another building. "This was the original club before we expanded it and made a bigger one. It's empty and waiting for demolition."

The perfect place to hide someone. I still wondered how Otis got passed the magical security and enchantment.

That question was answered as soon as Tania opened the door to the abandoned building. "Lork! What are you doing here?"

The male fae stared at Tania with wide eyes. His mouth did a good impression of a fish before he said, "T. I thought you were off tonight."

She folded her arms and glared at him. "Not asking again."

There was power behind her words, and I wished I had some popcorn to enjoy the show.

Lork glanced at each of us. "I was double checking if everything was out of the building. The demolition crew called and said they'd be out in the morning."

My heart dropped to my feet. I thanked the Universe for bring us to this building tonight. Now that the door was open, I could smell her. Julie was in there.

Felix must have come to the same conclusion I did because he pushed past me and Tania to get inside. When Lork stepped in his path, Felix growled and grabbed the male by the throat. "Where is she?"

Lork started to shake, and he pointed to the back left corner. Felix dropped him like last week's trash and flashed to Julie who was chained up in a dark corner of the room.

I rushed to her and fell to my knees. "Julie."

She looked at me and smiled weakly. "You shouldn't be here."

"Neither should you."

She shrugged and held up her arm, revealing the metal cuff and chain. "Iron. It makes the fae weak."

Felix gripped the cuff and broke it off, then worked on the ones on her other wrist and her ankles. Julie sagged in his arms as he rose to his feet, cradling her to him.

Julie only stayed cuddled up to him for a few seconds before she wiggled to be put down. Reluctantly, Felix lowered her to her feet, but he didn't leave her side. Julie met Tania's gaze and said, "Lork helped Otis."

Just then the door to the building flew open and Otis stepped inside with at least five demons backing him up. The crap just got real.

CHAPTER FOURTEEN

"Get Mattie and Julie out of here," Felix ordered and lowered his fangs.

I really didn't know who he was talking to, nor did I care. I wasn't leaving. Felix, Talon, Anya, and Julie were my family, and I wasn't about to hide out while they fight the bad guy.

"Not happening." I pulled out my phone and sent a text to Xel with the pics of his demons with Stacy's killer. "I called back up."

As soon as the words left my mouth, the demon king and a few of his enforcers materialized in front of us. Xel tipped his Stetson in greeting. Who wore a cowboy hat to a fight? Apparently, the king of demons. "Felix and I can handle it from here."

I really didn't want to leave them with the crazy

human guy. I could tell that Julie didn't either. But I did have a question for Otis. "Why did you do it?"

Otis snarled in disgust at us. "Because of him." He pointed at Felix.

Okay, that made a lot of sense. Not. "Felix made you do it?" I laughed and added, "How is that, *human*?"

Otis curled his lip at me. "I know who you are. You are just like the rest of the family. Superiority complex. You think you are better than any of us."

I looked around because I wasn't sure who he was talking to. What did he mean by the family? "Explain."

Otis rolled his eyes. "You're a Valgard and don't deny it."

I gasped and expected the others to as well. When they didn't, I looked at Felix and Julie. This was not new news to them. Hmm. We would be talking about that when we got home. For sure.

The Valgards were the oldest magical family. They were sorcerers and were all killed according to Xel and Anya.

"And who are you? I know you're not completely human," I countered.

"I'm your fourth cousin."

Well, then. I had no way of verifying if that was

the truth or not. It didn't matter if he really was my cousin. He kidnapped my best friend and killed an innocent girl.

And Otis wasn't done with gloating on all his great knowledge and evil plot. "My mother, wife, and kids were slaughtered by vampires." He pointed to Felix, "He gave the order."

I slowly turned my head to look at Felix. As usual the vampire leader didn't deny or confirm Otis's accusations. The answer was not important. My intuition said I could trust Felix and it was never wrong.

Turning back to Otis, I said, "Why did you kill the female demon?"

Otis laughed like an insane person. *If the shoe fits.* Then he said, "She wasn't the first. I wouldn't have killed your friend over there but thought she was better use to bring you all into my trap."

Oh great, what did the crazy little man do?

The floor under our feet started to shake and the glass in the windows shatter. Talon moved to stand in front of me and I didn't understand why until saw Otis lifted his arm and pointed a gun right at me. I screamed and thrust my arms out. With my right hand, I pushed Talon out of the way, using my super strength. At the same time, I pushed all my power into the other hand, aiming for Otis.

Felix and Xel yelled something before my friends dropped to the floor while my magic created a power blast that sent Otis and his demon minions flying backwards.

As fast as it happened, it was done. Silence settled in around me and for a while I didn't move. *What just happened?* I'd never experienced that amount of magic inside me.

We are bad ass! My wolf pranced around under my skin like she was proud of the carnage we caused.

Talon touched my shoulder. "Are you okay?"

"Physically, yes."

Xel moved into my line of sight and stared into my eyes. After a few moments, he stepped back and broke the eye contact. "You must be prepared for what's to come. It's not going to be easy."

"What are you talking about?"

"All will be revealed soon." Xel nodded to Felix. "Take them home, I'll help Tania clean up here."

Felix directed us out of the building and to our vehicles.

Instead of going to my apartment, we all stopped off at Talon's Coffee House. A rich, creamy coffee was a great idea. Talon gave me a cranberry orange muffin. When I took the first bite of it, I felt relaxed and revived at the same time.

We sat at a table near the back for privacy even though it wasn't too busy this time of night. For a long while no one spoke. That was driving me crazy. "Am I really a sorceress? A Valgard?"

Felix and Julie nodded. Julie took my hand and squeezed. "Your mother came to Felix shortly after your birth and asked for protection in case something happened to her."

My chest ached at the mentioned of my mom. She knew this would happen one day, yet she never told me. "Why didn't she tell me?"

"Elizabeth didn't expect to leave you so soon. We already had things set in motion to bring you here, but things got complicated. Liz's death was sudden, and your uncle covered it up and kept you on a very short leash." Felix worked his jaw, then continued. "I couldn't go in and pull you out without Roger getting suspicious. We don't need him digging into who your father is."

Julie added, "Liz said she never told anyone who your father was. The less Roger knew the safer you were."

"But she told you two?"

They nodded and Julie said, "I moved to Abbotsford to keep an eye on you and make sure your uncle didn't get any bright ideas."

Did they think Roger killed my mom? I don't see that happening because even though Roger was a rogue and meaner than pissed off cat, he was also a coward.

"What do we do now?"

Anya broke her silence. "You will join the Seattle Coven and train with me, Talon, and my mom on using and concealing your powers. That blast you let off back there had unlocked them."

Yeah, I knew that. I felt the magic roaming wild inside me. My wolf was playing with the threads of power, making my body feel like a live wire. I would definitely have to meditate and ground myself when I got home.

"Anything else?" I said on a yawn. Talon put something in my coffee.

"Chamomile," my sneaky mate whispered in my ear. That explained it. "Plus, you are drained after releasing all that power."

"I guess," I said, then finished off my coffee and muffin.

Felix tapped his fingers on the table. "We'll take this day by day. There will be people searching for you now. That power you released was like a beacon."

That was what Xel meant with his creepy cryptic message at the abandoned building behind the club.

Julie patted my hand. "We got your back all the way. You will never be alone again."

I knew that. I had a new group of friends that were fast becoming my family. We may not be blood, but we looked out for one another. That was the best type of family to have.

After Talon cleaned off the table we went home.

As soon as I entered the lobby of Hex Towers, I felt a familiar energy. I glanced around the lobby until my eyes landed on a tall, slender man standing by the fountain to our left. We locked gazes and my wolf growled. She didn't like this man.

He approached, putting Talon and Anya on alert. Felix and Julie had hung back at the coffee house for some alone time. They needed it. I'll have her tomorrow.

Focusing on the man who now stood a few feet from me, I asked, "Can I help you?"

A slow smiled curved his lips. "No, but I can help you."

Umm, I didn't think so. "Who are you?"

He held out his hand. "Svafar Valgard. Your father."

Don't miss Matty's next adventure in The Midlife Shift, book 2 in Packless in Seattle.

Stay up to date on new releases, exclusive cover reveals, giveaways, and much more by joining Lia's mailing list. http://www. subscribepage.com/authorliadavis.newsletter

USA Today bestselling author Lia Davis spends most of her time writing racy romance and witty women's fiction, the majority of which takes place in fantasy worlds full of magic and mayhem. She prides herself on her ability to craft strong and sassy heroines, emotionally intelligent alpha heroes, and rich, expansive universes that readers want to visit again and again.

She is the mastermind behind the bestselling Ashwood Falls Series and the co-author of the beloved Witching After Forty Series.

She currently resides in Florida where she's working on her very own happily-ever-after with her supportive husband and spends her free time doting on a pack of feisty felines and her loving family.

Follow Lia on Social Media

Website: http://www.authorliadavis.com/

Newsletter: http://www.subscribepage.com/authorliadavis.newsletter
Facebook author fan page: https://www.facebook.com/novelsbylia/
Facebook Fan Club: https://www.facebook.com/groups/LiaDavisFanClub/
Twitter: https://twitter.com/novelsbylia
Instagram: https://www.instagram.com/authorliadavis/
BookBub: https://www.bookbub.com/authors/lia-davis
Pinterest: http://www.pinterest.com/liadavis35/
Goodreads: http://www.goodreads.com/author/show/5829989.Lia_Davis

Check out the official Davis Raynes Merch store on Etsy: https://www.etsy.com/shop/davisraynesmerch

Paranormal Women's Fiction

Witching After Forty (Co-written with L.A. Boruff)

Fanged After Forty (Co-written with L.A. Boruff)

Shifting Through Midlife (Co-written with L.A. Boruff and Lacey Carter)

Packless in Seattle

Paranormal Romance Series

Shifters of Ashwood Falls

Bears of Blackrock

Dragons of Ares

Gods and Dragons

Dark Scales Division (Co-written with Kerry Adrienne)

Shifting Magick Trilogy

The Divinities

Witches of Rose Lake

Coven's End (Co-written with L.A. Boruff)

Academy's Rise (Co-written with L.A. Boruff)

www.ingramcontent.com/pod-product-compliance
Lightning Source LLC
Chambersburg PA
CBHW071328140726
47996CB00005B/1878